The Forg

Harrison Kincaid—and his sister, Nessa, spent all of July and August on Summer Island with their parents. In his thirties Harrison married Simone and became the CEO of his family-owned communications business based out of Seattle.

Aidan Wythe—Raised by his mother in Seattle, Aidan has been Harrison's best friend for as long as he can remember. They went to Yale together and Aidan is Harrison's right-hand man at Kincaid Communications.

Emerson Cotley—A local on Summer Island, Emerson took over the family landscaping business after his parents were killed in a car accident.

Jennifer March—Her family owns the Lavender Farm Bed and Breakfast on Summer Island. She and Simone were best friends.

Gabe Brooke—Gabe owns a real estate business on Summer Island, as well as the local newspaper. He married Harrison's sister, Nessa, after Harrison married Simone.

Simone DeRosier—A renowned jazz singer and pianist, Simone started spending her holidays with her father on Summer Island when she was fourteen years old. She coined the phrase "Forget-Me-Not Friend" in her first Grammy Award-winning hit.

Dear Reader,

In this book I'm taking you back to Summer Island, a locale I introduced this June in the Signature Select Saga novel, *You Made Me Love You.*

I first dreamed of Summer Island when my family and I spent a holiday with my sister's family on Saltspring Island. We had a grand time lazing on the ocean shore, hiking in the rolling hills and kayaking on the becalmed sea. One of the highlights for my city-slicker daughters was setting traps for crabs with my brother-in-law Gord. I couldn't believe it when those picky little children actually ate them, too!

As we explored the Gulf Coast island, I knew I had to write a book about this place one day. No, not just a book, a three-book series. I wasn't sure what the stories would be about, but I started with a picture in my head....

Five friends sitting around a bonfire on the beach late at night. They're roasting marshmallows and drinking and kidding around with the ease of kids who've known each other all their lives. Then someone new asks to join their group...and their futures are altered forever.

I hope you enjoy this story. The concluding book of this trilogy, *Secrets Between Them,* will be available in October from Harlequin Superromance. Be sure to watch for it.

If you would like to write or send e-mail, I would be delighted to hear from you through my Web site at www.cjcarmichael.com. Or send mail to the following Canadian address: #1754–246 Stewart Green, S.W., Calgary, Alberta, T3H 3C8, Canada.

Sincerely,

C.J. Carmichael

A BABY
BETWEEN THEM
C.J. Carmichael

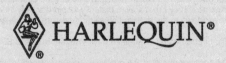

TORONTO • NEW YORK • LONDON
AMSTERDAM • PARIS • SYDNEY • HAMBURG
STOCKHOLM • ATHENS • TOKYO • MILAN • MADRID
PRAGUE • WARSAW • BUDAPEST • AUCKLAND

ISBN-13: 978-0-373-78101-0
ISBN-10:   0-373-78101-6

A BABY BETWEEN THEM

Copyright © 2006 by Carla Daum.

www.eHarlequin.com

Printed in U.S.A.

Books by C.J. Carmichael

HARLEQUIN SUPERROMANCE

SIGNATURE SELECT SAGA

PROLOGUE

Summer Island

AIDAN WYTHE DIDN'T make friends easily, so when the new girl suddenly appeared on the beach in the moonlight, his instinct was to nod politely, and then turn away. His friends Harrison Kincaid and Gabe Brooke, however, reacted quite differently. Harrison scrambled to his feet. Gabe offered her a drink.

"That's a good fire." The girl moved closer to the bonfire, holding out a hand as if she were cold.

She was beautiful. No, more than that. Stunning was a better word.

"It's even warmer over here." Gabe patted the surface of the log he was sitting on in invitation.

The girl hesitated. "Are you sure I'm not interrupting?"

"Yeah, actually, you are," Aidan said. Something about her made him uneasy. Just because Harrison and Gabe were already drooling didn't mean they should invite her to join them. The five of them had been having a great time without her. Aidan looked to Jennifer for support, but even she was frowning at his comment.

"Don't mind him," Jennifer said.

"Yeah," Gabe added. "Aidan was bit by a rabid dog when he was a kid. He's never been the same."

Aidan told Gabe what to do with himself. But everyone else laughed. And the new girl sat down.

"My dad and I are here for the summer. My name's Simone. Simone DeRosier."

Gabe and Harrison both repeated her name as if to make sure they would never forget it. What idiots. They were still gawking as if they'd never seen a pretty girl before.

"I'm Gabe Brooke. I live here on the island, and these are my friends." Gabe went around the fire, pointing as he spoke each of their names: "Emerson and Jennifer are locals, too. Aidan and Harrison are from Seattle."

"Hi, Simone. It's good to meet you." Harrison leaned closer and offered his hand.

Aidan cringed. *God, Harrison. Shaking hands was what grown-ups did. Not sixteen-year-old guys who were just hanging out on the beach.*

But Simone smiled as brightly as if Harrison was the coolest dude she'd ever met.

"It's nice to meet you, too, Harrison." She turned to girl beside him. "Is this your girlfriend?"

Jennifer laughed. "No, we're just friends. We're *all* friends." She pushed her blond hair off her shoulders. "My parents own a bed-and-breakfast on the north end."

"My folks have a landscaping business," Emerson added. "We live on Oyster Bay, just a few miles from here."

Finally Simone's eyes settled on Aidan. "That leaves you, Aidan. Where do you stay when you're on the island? Do you rent a place in town?"

He didn't answer, so Harrison filled in.

"He and his mom own the cottage across from our place. Aidan and I go to school together in Seattle. We're planning to be roommates when we go to Yale."

"Cool. Have you guys known each other long?"

"Basically all our lives," Emerson said. "Our moms used to bring us to this beach when we were little kids."

"How lucky for you." Simone sounded genuinely envious. "Well, thanks, Aidan, for letting me barge in on the party like this."

Why would she thank *him*, when he was probably the only one who didn't want her here? He looked up from the fire and scowled. He didn't care if she knew he didn't like her. Harrison and Gabe were fools. Their tongues were going to be caked with sand if they didn't shove them back into their mouths pretty soon.

Simone wrapped her arms around her knees and leaned forward. "So what do you like to do?"

"Volleyball. Swim. Hang out," Jennifer said. "How about you?"

"I like those things, too." She paused a moment. "Do any of you sing?"

"Around the campfire, you mean?" Aidan's voice dripped with scorn. He'd known he wouldn't like this girl. "Not since I was a Boy Scout, when I was ten."

"But then you're tone-deaf, Aidan." Harrison offered the insult with the casual air of a lifelong friend. "My mother makes me and my sister, Nessa, take piano lessons. How about you, Simone? Do you sing?"

She nodded and faked a shy look. She didn't fool Aidan, though. He knew she was dying for the chance to show off. Sure enough, less than a minute later, Gabe and Harrison had convinced her to sing for them.

She surprised Aidan by picking an old-fashioned jazz tune. And then she surprised them all by how impossibly wonderful she sounded.

When she stopped, Aidan couldn't think of even one cutting thing to say. In fact, no one spoke at all for several seconds. And then, suddenly, everyone was gushing.

"You're unbelievable…."

"Are you sure you're not a professional…?"

"I've never heard anyone…"

Simone sat back on the log and soaked it

all up. For a moment her eyes settled on his and he saw the self-satisfaction in them.

You witch, he thought. She was going to mess up everything this summer. He just knew it.

CHAPTER ONE

Summer Island, twenty-three years later

AIDAN WYTHE NOTICED the rental car parked in front of the house where he'd be staying for the next three weeks, but at first he didn't think anything of it.

Twenty minutes ago he'd driven off the ferry, officially starting his first real vacation in several years. Now he pulled his convertible into the driveway, cut the engine and just sat for a moment.

Here he was, back in Canada, on Summer Island.

He closed his eyes and focused on the scent of the ocean and the feel of the gulf breeze in his hair. Memories, both good and bad, teased his mind like the wind. No matter how many times he returned as an adult, it was always his childhood that came back to him first.

Most of his recollections were of happy hours spent beachcombing, swimming and picnicking with his friends. The five of them had had their disagreements, but they were always minor and had been patched quickly and with little resentment.

All that had changed, however, the summer they turned sixteen—when Simone DeRosier joined their circle. It was that summer that innocence had been lost and the seeds of obsession and evil that would tear the group apart were planted.

Aidan rubbed his forehead, opened his eyes. Just thinking of the famous jazz singer—dead now, murdered by one of their own—stirred up his old resentments. He didn't want to hang on to them, but still…

Everything had been so easy before Simone arrived on the scene. Unfortunately, Aidan had been the only one to see that she was trouble. He wasn't sure what had tipped him off. Her uncommon beauty, a certain look in her eyes, the stunning power in her voice when she'd first sung for the five of them.

She'd instantly captivated Harrison, Gabe, Emerson and Jennifer, and for years after that she'd played them off against each other, all the while pretending that they were the best friends in the world.

She'd even immortalized their friendship with a song: "Forget Me Not, Old Friend" had been a big hit and had won her a Grammy. From that moment on, the press—and eventually even the five of them—had referred to themselves as the Forget-Me-Not gang.

Personally, Aidan hated the label.

Not that it mattered anymore. There was no gang left to speak of. Not with Simone and Emerson dead, and Harrison and Gabe not speaking to each other. Gabe hated Harrison because he was the one Simone had married. Harrison hated Gabe for seducing and marrying his baby sister, Nessa, then making her so miserable that she'd finally divorced him.

With friends like those, who needed enemies?

Aidan sighed, then slipped off his sunglasses and tossed them on the dash. From the driver's seat of his Mustang convertible, he contemplated the gracious home that had belonged to the Kincaid family for three generations. Through decades of upheaval this house was the one thing that hadn't really changed.

The old Victorian was a stalwart structure, built with its back to the sea, the broad front verandah providing an open welcome to family and guests alike. A Gothic-style second-story turret, where Simone had once composed her music, overlooked an ancient cedar forest that formed the heart of the island.

Much as Aidan wanted to remember the place as it had seemed to him in his childhood—warm, inviting, almost magical—he couldn't help recalling that this was where Simone DeRosier had been murdered.

And now he was supposed to vacation here. To relax. Just because his office staff thought he was overstressed from too much work.

He jumped out of the convertible without opening the door, then went round to the back and removed his luggage from the trunk. He paused and glanced farther down the road to Pebble Beach. Wooden stairs led from a modest parking lot to a naturally protected cove. He remembered summer nights sitting by a bonfire on the beach, then later strolling along the boardwalk that led all the way back to town. He, Harrison, Emerson, Gabe and Jennifer had had a lot of fun in those pre-Simone days.

Aidan hefted an expansive duffel bag over his shoulder, then had another cursory glance at the rental car parked next to the driveway. Must be someone visiting the yoga studio across the road. He dug Harrison's key out of his jeans pocket and headed for the front door.

Last time he'd been on the island—about a year ago—Harrison had been in residence. He'd been investigating the circumstances of Simone's death, and then, along the way, he'd fallen in love with his real estate agent, Justine Melbourne. No one had been more surprised than Aidan when Harrison and Justine succeeded in proving Simone's death had not been suicide, but murder.

Harrison could be fiercely tenacious when he wanted something. Like this stupid holiday idea. Harrison had all but packed

Aidan's bags and filled his car with gas, he'd been that anxious to get his friend out of the office in Seattle. Just because Aidan had called Harrison while he was sleeping with a great idea for a merger target.

"It's three o'clock in the morning, Aidan. You need to get a life."

But it had been a great idea….

Never mind, maybe he had been guilty of overworking this last little while. But he had to, didn't he? Otherwise, if he weren't careful, he'd be thinking about things that were better forgotten.

Aidan dropped his bag to the porch floor. The wooden boards looked freshly stained. The entire property was well-maintained. He glanced back at his car, wondering if he should put up the roof. But the clear sky held no hint of a summer storm.

What had brought him back to this place for his holiday? Sure Harrison had offered the use of his house, but money wasn't an object—Aidan could have traveled anywhere in the world. It was almost as if he couldn't stay away, as if the island had laid a claim on him, a claim that had to be settled.

Gloomy thoughts, man. You're supposed to be on holiday, remember?

He inserted his key into the lock, then pushed the door open. Immediately, he was accosted by an acrid smell. A second later, a loud crash sounded from the back of the house where the kitchen was.

What the hell? Harrison had told him a cleaning crew would have the place stocked and ready for his arrival, but this couldn't be them, could it?

And then it hit him. The driver of that rental car wasn't at the yoga studio, after all.

RAE CORDELL HAD READ the instructions on the plastic wrapper that was now lying on the counter. It wasn't that complicated. "Remove from packaging and place loaf on a cookie sheet in a prewarmed 325 degree oven. Bake for thirty to thirty-five minutes, until the bread is golden brown and sounds hollow when tapped."

Yes, it had all sounded very simple. But Rae knew that if anyone could screw up baking a loaf of oven-ready bread, it would be her.

She peeked in the oven, and the yeasty aroma that greeted her made her gag. Oh, God. She had to get to a washroom. Quick.

Just hours ago, she'd been craving a slice of thick bread, slathered in butter. Now, the scent of the baking dough made her ill.

Rae kneeled over the toilet, and when she was done, mopped off her face and then checked her reflection in the mirror above the sink.

What was wrong with her? Why couldn't she do the things that seemed to come to other women so easily? Like cooking. And being pregnant.

Everyone knew morning sickness ended after the first trimester. Yet here she was, well into her eighth month. And the nausea still struck without warning and often at the most inopportune times. Like during Thursday afternoon staff meetings. And business dinners with important financiers. No wonder she'd been invited to take an expenses-paid vacation until the baby was born.

Oh, Harrison's wife had been very sweet on the phone. Justine had said that since she and her husband were planning to spend August in Seattle, their summer home would be vacant. Why didn't Rae take the opportunity and allow herself a well-deserved vacation?

Justine's suggestion had been echoed by the executive assistant who worked under Rae at the Pittsburgh office of Kincaid Communications. The human relations director in Seattle had called for a "personal chat" and so had the VPs for Finance and Marketing. In fact, Rae had heard from almost everyone at the corporation except for the one person who really counted: her direct boss, acting CEO Aidan Wythe.

Rae placed her hands awkwardly over the huge mound of her abdomen. *The man who got me in this predicament in the first place.*

Her pregnancy had been common knowledge for at least the past three months—it wasn't the sort of news one could hide forever—and she'd spent weeks dreading the prospect of hearing from him. But he hadn't come to the Pittsburgh office in all that time. He hadn't even called. Finally, it dawned on her that he didn't intend to face up to the situation. Knowing men, Rae figured that he'd probably convinced himself someone else was the father.

Well, Rae had no interest in dissuading him of that notion. In fact, the more she reflected on her situation, the more she came to think that Aidan's disinterest worked perfectly with her own plans.

This way, she didn't need to consider anyone's needs but hers and the baby's.

The timer on the oven sounded again, and Rae was forced to head back to the kitchen. As soon as she stepped out of the bathroom, she knew something was wrong.

The bread was burning. She ran to the oven, slipped on oven mitts and opened the door. The top of the loaf was scorched black. As she pulled it out, her thumb pressed through a worn spot on the oven mitt.

Yikes! She dropped the pan and it clattered loudly against the granite-topped counter. It was in the ensuing silence that she heard the footsteps. Someone was in the house and heading her way.

Rae knew she'd locked the door after her morning walk. Was she about to be robbed? Raped? She reached for the hot pan, ready to hurl it if she had to. As she closed her gloved hands over her improvised weapon, a man stepped into the kitchen.

"Oh!" She stifled her scream at the moment of recognition. Damn it, this wasn't possible, was it? Separated from her by a ten-foot, granite-topped island, Aidan Wythe looked almost as startled as Rae felt.

"Aidan?" She spoke the name as if his identity might be in doubt, but of course it wasn't. Damn him, he looked good—even with windblown hair, and dressed in a casual T-shirt and jeans rather than his usual Armani suit and tie.

Oh, my Lord.

She dropped the pan to the countertop for the second time. Fighting an urge to run from the room, she gripped the counter for balance.

Why wasn't he saying anything? What was he doing here? Rae swallowed, and drew in a long breath. The staccato pounding of her heart made her feel as if she'd just run up a long flight of stairs.

"This can't be happening." She closed her eyes, then opened them, hoping this apparition would disappear. Big surprise—it didn't.

Aidan crossed his arms. Frowned. "What are you doing here?"

"Shouldn't that be my line?" Must be the baby she was carrying, but she was having a hard time catching her breath. She leaned a little harder against the counter, trying not to wish that she looked slightly more presentable.

She was still flushed from her morning walk, and she hadn't changed from the baggy T-shirt and shorts that she wore for exercise. Surely no one expected an extremely pregnant woman to look that good, anyway.

Not that it mattered. This was Aidan Wythe. The man she'd thought was so different…so sensitive, so deep. And he'd turned out to be the biggest jerk of all.

"Harrison told me his house was vacant for the month of August." As Aidan spoke, his gaze raked over Rae, and she could almost hear him listing all the flaws he must be seeing. Messy hair that hadn't been washed in days, no makeup, terrible clothes.

Whereas Aidan looked...absolutely delicious. More handsome than ever, not to mention calm and collected, even though—as Rae now understood—he hadn't expected to see her here, either.

Well, that explained one mystery. She should have known he wouldn't have been *looking* for her.

"Funny," she said. "That's exactly what Justine told *me*."

Aidan blinked, surprise registering in his enigmatic, dark eyes. Finally, he broke the visual connection and crossed the room to the windows. The Pacific Ocean, deceptively calm on this late-summer day, dominated the view through all three picture windows that ran the length of the combined kitchen and dining area.

Rae stayed where she was, watching him push his hands into the pockets of his jeans, and trying not to admire the way the dark denim outlined slim hips, long legs, tight ass.

Ah, hell, it wasn't fair. Aidan had never looked better. Shouldn't men like him come marked in some way to warn innocent women of the potential danger? He hadn't asked her how she was feeling, hadn't even acknowledged the fact that she was pregnant. He really was a cad.

Now she glanced at the spot where he'd been standing earlier and saw a very large duffel bag. And suddenly the ramifications of the problem before them increased significantly.

"You came here for a vacation?"

"Yes." He swung round to face her again. "How long are you planning to stay?"

Rae looked at him, incredulous. He had to be the most self-centered man on the planet. "Why, until the baby's born, of course."

Aidan's hands dropped to his side. His face went blank. "Baby?"

Stepping out from behind the island, Rae rounded her hands over her large belly. Good grief, his face. It was almost as if…

"Oh, my God. Rae, why didn't you tell me?"

CHAPTER TWO

"YOU DIDN'T KNOW?" Rae's voice, usually so strong and confident, gave out in a squeak at the end of her question.

Aidan couldn't find the words to answer her. He was in shock. Her belly was huge. Enormous. She looked as though she was ready to pop at any second. He tore his gaze from her middle and gave the rest of her a closer look. In contrast with her belly, her arms and legs seemed abnormally skinny. Once, she'd had curves in all the right places. Now, her curves were definitely in all the *wrong* places.

"Rae, when did this happen?"

She placed her hands, covered in quilted oven mitts, on her hips. "You know damn well when it happened. Eight months ago, in that stupid hotel room in Philadelphia where we were supposed to be preparing our presentation for the Triumph merger."

He covered his face with one hand. Groaned. Eight months... Yes, that took them right back to the night he'd spent with her. He'd known then that he was making a mistake. But he'd had no idea just what a whopper it would turn out to be.

"Why haven't I heard about this? You never called."

Her gaze focused in on him like a laser beam. "You made it perfectly clear my calls weren't welcome when you banished me to Pittsburgh."

"Banished? That was a *promotion,* Rae." Holding out his hand, he ticked off the reasons on his fingers. "You got more money, more responsibility, a step up the corporate ladder."

Rae shook her head, releasing more strands of wild, dark hair from her loose ponytail. "Sure, Aidan. And you didn't have to go to work every day and face the woman you'd made the mistake of sleeping with. Be honest and admit the truth. You sent me to Pittsburgh to get rid of me."

Her words infuriated him and he had to struggle to reply calmly. "Not true."

"If you weren't trying to avoid me, then why did you stop making monthly visits to Pittsburgh once I was made divisional VP?"

"I trusted you to handle the job."

"Oh, really? And the switch from the conference phone calls you used to make to divisional VPs to group e-mails—that must have been another example of your great trust? It wasn't because you didn't want to hear the sound of my voice?"

"You're reading too much into all that. And forgetting how busy I've been, with Harrison out of the office so much…."

Since he'd married Justine, Harrison had started working eleven months of the year from here on Summer Island. It had fallen on Aidan, who'd been promoted and given a huge raise, to fill in the gaps.

"Right." She looked at him scornfully. "You've been busy. You haven't been avoiding face time with the employee you screwed. And when I say 'screwed,' of course I'm speaking literally *and* figuratively."

Aidan paced to the far corner of the room.

He needed space to think. He needed to be calm and rational. But every time he looked at Rae's enormous belly he felt as if he was about to have a panic attack.

Focus on something else for a minute. In front of him, the Kincaid china cabinet was filled with French Provincial serving dishes, teapots, ornaments. He felt like smashing the lot of them.

So much for calm and rational.

He turned to face Rae again. "What were you expecting me to do? We shouldn't have slept together. It was a mistake and we both should have known better." He let out a huge sigh of exasperation. "Because of my position of authority, I recognize that I shoulder the majority of the blame."

She blinked and her head jerked back a little, as if he'd slapped her.

What had he said wrong this time? Surely she couldn't deny that what they'd done had been ill-advised, to say the very least.

"Look, we're two ambitious people, who in a moment of weakness…" He paused, remembering that moment of weakness, and how truly incredible it had seemed at the time. That night he'd wanted her so badly that he hadn't cared about consequences. About *any* consequences. For the first time in his life he'd been so carried away that he hadn't used a condom.

He hadn't even asked if she was protected. Which, clearly, she hadn't been.

"Rae, even if you think I'm the biggest jerk in the world…"

"Sounds about right."

He decided to ignore that. "I still deserved to be told you were pregnant."

"Really? Why?"

Her answer stunned him. "Because I'm the father."

"So what? You contributed the sperm. Big deal." With her hands still covered in protective mitts, she picked up the pan and tipped the loaf of bread on it into the trash. "This smell is making me sick. Or maybe it's you. I'm not sure."

Fighting words, again. But throwing insults back and forth wasn't accomplishing anything. Aidan tried to see her side of the situation. "You've been through a lot. Maybe you've got reason to be upset with me. But at least you could have told me. Given me a chance."

"A chance to do what, Aidan? Marry me?" She took off the oven mitts. Tossed them to the counter, as if she were issuing some kind of challenge.

"Is that what you want?" he asked quietly.

"Jesus, Aidan!" she exploded again. "I don't even like you anymore. Why would I want to marry you?"

Okay, that hurt. But why? Wasn't this exactly the real reason he'd sent her away? So that their feelings for each other might cool to a point where they'd be able to continue their professional relationship without the risk of messy emotional entanglement?

"As the father, I have responsibilities. At the very minimum, there will be support payments." He pictured years and years of tidy monthly bills, and the thought of this obligation—which he was certainly capable of following through on—calmed him somewhat.

Rae crossed to the closest of the windows and opened it, allowing a fresh breeze into the room. Leaning her forehead against the frame, she fixed her attention on the ocean.

For a moment, Aidan admired the beauty of the woman. Rae had strong, compelling features, with thick, dark hair, rosy cheeks and a lush, wide mouth. Since the day he'd met her, he'd been attracted to Rae. Then, she'd been lean and fit, with small, high breasts and a curvy bottom he couldn't tear his gaze from. Now, he was surprised to find that her new shape held a certain fascination for him, too.

He was so focused on the picture she made, outlined against the bright sunlight outside, that he almost missed her next words.

"This baby won't need your support payments, Aidan."

He took a moment to process that. "I know you earn a good living and you're capable of handling everything on your own. But I can't let you. It isn't right. I'll pay my share. And I want to be involved in other ways, too."

That last bit startled him, as much as it obviously surprised Rae. She turned to him, her dark eyes narrowing skeptically.

When had he decided he wanted to be a father in a real sense? Aidan didn't know. But it was true. He wasn't going to walk away from this responsibility, no matter how much he didn't want it.

She glanced out the window again. "That won't be necessary. In fact, it won't even be possible."

So, he wasn't good enough for their baby. He wasn't surprised that she would think that. But what about financial support? Surely she didn't mean to turn her back on that, as well. "You don't want anything?"

"Not from you."

This should have filled him with relief. Instead, Aidan was furious. With her, and with himself. He clenched his fists, and asked himself what kind of man felt like shaking a pregnant woman? Because that was certainly his urge right now. He wanted to grab her by the shoulders and *make* her look at him. He jammed his hands back into his pockets.

"You're just saying that to hurt me."

"I'm saying it because it's true. You won't have any responsibilities for me or anyone else."

"But…"

"Aidan, listen." She spoke sharply, her eyes flashing. "You won't need to look after this baby, and neither will I. I'm not keeping it."

FOR THE SECOND TIME that afternoon, Aidan looked utterly stunned, and Rae knew he wasn't faking it. Even Johnny Depp couldn't act that well. Still, it was hard to believe he hadn't heard she was pregnant. Although they worked in different cities, there were constant phone and e-mail communications between the various branch offices and subsidiaries of Kincaid Communications. Surely *someone* would have told him?

But maybe everyone had assumed he knew. That she'd told him. Because the rumor mill had figured out their night together and, from that, had worked out the most likely reason she'd been banished to Pittsburgh.

And she *had* been banished, no matter how many times Aidan described it as a promotion. All acquisitions and mergers were handled out of the Seattle office, and that had been the reason Harrison had brought her into the organization in the first place. To handle those sorts of special deals.

Frankly, the everyday business she supervised in the Pittsburgh office, even though it did amount technically to a promotion in terms of salary and title, bored her silly. Aidan had to understand that. He was the same way. He thrived on the chase, just as much as she did.

It was one of the things she'd liked most about him, one of the reasons she'd thought maybe she'd finally met her match, in the romantic sense of the word. She'd never been attracted to men who weren't as smart as she was, as driven and competitive.

Aidan had been all of these things. In addition, Rae had thought he was honorable and principled, too. That was the way he did business, at least.

But he'd slept with her, and then he'd shown her the door. Which made him a bitter disappointment…not the man she'd thought he was, at all.

Clearly still reeling from the emotional one-two punch Rae had just delivered, Aidan opened the sliding doors that led to the patio.

He walked to the railing and, after a moment's thought, she followed him there. This view had been a solace to her over the few days she'd been here. Now she gazed over the becalmed sea and wondered what it must look like during the winter storms. This would be a bleak place in December, she suspected.

"Why are you giving up the baby?"

"I would have thought that was obvious."

In profile, Aidan's chin was set, his mouth drawn in a long, disapproving line.

"I'm a career woman. Not the mothering sort. The baby will be happier with a mom *and* a dad. Parents who really want it."

His gaze brushed against hers for a moment, conveying disbelief. "And you don't? Want it?"

"Of course not." What was he thinking? "You can't be suggesting I became pregnant on purpose?"

"No."

"That's good. Because I didn't. Men aren't the only ones who can get carried away by…lust." She chose that word because he, like most men, believed in lust and understood lust.

Whereas for her that night had been about magic and once-in-a-lifetime opportunities, but she'd be damned before she'd admit to *him* that she'd ever held such idealistic notions.

"You don't think it will be hard? To give up the baby after it's born?"

"Naturally it will be hard. This whole pregnancy business has been hard! Nine months has never seemed so long."

Aidan reached out a hand to touch her, then withdrew it. "I'm sorry, Rae. You've been through so much. And coped with all of it on your own."

She closed her eyes, hating the fact that he sounded so sincere and caring. He wasn't really the kind of man a woman could count on. It was just that every now and then he happened to say exactly the right thing to make her crumble.

"When did you find out?" he asked softly.

"I suspected I was pregnant soon after the move." Her breasts had been so tender and she'd been atypically tired; a drugstore kit had confirmed the news, all too easily.

"And you never considered...termination?"

"Why? Is that what you wish I'd done?"

A light shifted in his eyes and he made a noise of reconciliation. "Sorry, I forgot. You were raised Catholic."

She'd told him so much about herself on that one night together. Far too much. They'd talked for hours, in between their lovemaking sessions. She'd felt as if she'd found her soul mate. He'd been so easy to confide in.

Later, she'd been mortified to realize that she had been the one doing most of the talking. She'd wondered if he'd even been listening.

Apparently he had. At least to some of her ramblings.

He was right about the Catholic upbringing, at any rate. She rarely went to church anymore and her mother had been dead for years, but still those childhood teachings rang in Rae's ears.

So, no, abortion hadn't been the right choice for her.

"Has it been tough, Rae? Were you sick at the beginning?"

"Yes, and I still get sick now, even though all the books say the nauseous stage is supposed to end after the first few months."

She turned her back to the railing and leaned against it. The wind in her hair was refreshing. What had possessed her to try baking a loaf of bread in this heat?

"It's no fun looking like a house, either," she continued. "Or having to drink all that milk, which I hate, by the way. Lately, I've had the worst heartburn. And just this week my feet have become so swollen I can only squeeze them into one pair of sandals."

She saw him look down at her bare feet. In the past, she'd kept her toenails painted all the time—no matter what the season. But now they looked terrible. Even clipping them was difficult.

"Basically, being pregnant is rough. Anyone who says they like it must be crazy."

Aidan listened to all her complaints without saying a word and she wondered what he was thinking. Was he judging her—and finding her lacking? There had to be something wrong with a woman who didn't like being pregnant and didn't even want to keep her own baby. Maybe he'd sensed this deficiency in her all along. Perhaps that was why he'd exiled her to Pittsburgh.

"Do Justine and Harrison know you're pregnant?"

His question surprised her, but she nodded. "Sure." Harrison had made a trip to the Pittsburgh office a month ago and Justine and Autumn had come with him. It was shortly after that visit that Justine had called her with the offer to use this house for the month of August.

Aidan rubbed his chin, thoughtfully. "So we were set up."

"What are you talking about?"

"You told me Justine invited you to use this house, right?"

"Yes."

"Well, Harrison extended the same invitation to me."

"He did?" She thought of the duffel bag Aidan had brought inside. It was big. Obviously, he wasn't here for a weekend jaunt. "So...what are we going to do?"

"Under the circumstances, we can't stay under the same roof. Since you were here first, I'll find lodgings elsewhere."

She stared at him, wondering why his oh-so-rational plan didn't sound at all appealing to her. It must be the hormones scrambling her thinking.

"I'll be out of here as soon as possible, Rae."

"Good. The sooner, the better."

She tried to deliver her parting line with as much scorn as she could summon. Then she hurried inside, because damned if she didn't feel as if she was about to cry.

CHAPTER THREE

AIDAN WATCHED RAE'S rushed exit from the patio. She was clearly upset and he knew he should follow her and try to calm her down.

But he wasn't in any shape to help anyone right now. He held up his right hand. Sure enough, it was trembling.

Rae Cordell was pregnant with his baby.

He could *not* believe it.

His life plans had never involved getting married or having a child. Woman were too distracting. He'd learned that lesson at age sixteen, watching his friends make fools of themselves over Simone.

He'd wanted none of it for himself. Women were great, as long as you kept the upper hand. If you found that power slipping away, the smart thing to do was to back away immediately and find someone safer.

As he had backed away from Rae. Just one night together had been too much. He'd woken in a panic, knowing he'd made a terrible mistake. It wasn't just that they worked together. He recognized something in Rae that he'd seen in Simone, too.

Like Simone, Rae had a natural ability to command attention. Call it confidence or charisma, or whatever the hell you wanted. Rae wasn't a performer like Simone, but she still had star quality.

He'd wanted her the first time he'd met her. That on its own had signaled trouble, and so he'd tried to convince Harrison that the company didn't need Rae Cordell. But Harrison was concerned about Aidan's workload. He'd insisted they hang on to Rae, and so Aidan had been trapped. He'd done his best to keep one-on-one encounters with her to a minimum.

But the Triumph merger had undone all his best intentions. Late nights, last-minute negotiations and an out-of-town meeting had all added up to an impossible situation. One he hadn't been strong enough to resist.

The morning after, he'd panicked. He'd

slipped out of the hotel room without show-ering and caught an early flight to Seattle. Once back at the office, he'd immediately started working on damage control.

All the while, he'd berated himself. Why had he slept with her in the first place? He'd gone against all his principles. And presum-ing Rae had the contraceptives covered had to be one of the dumbest moves he'd ever made. Next to the night his mother died…

No. Don't go there now.

Aidan rubbed the back of his neck, wincing at the thought of what Rae must have gone through these past months. She'd already shared some of the physical indigni-ties of pregnancy…but what about the emo-tional burden?

Was she as blasé as she sounded about giving up the baby?

And what about the situation at work? He'd bet she hadn't told anyone who the father of the baby was. But he guessed someone had figured it out. Which meant the entire company knew by now.

Everyone but him.

How was it that he hadn't heard the

rumors? Aidan thought back to a few occasions when he'd walked into an office or a meeting room and encountered a sudden, uncomfortable silence.

Well, of course no one had said anything to him. He was the boss. No one had dared.

Anyway, they must have assumed he knew. That Rae would have told him.

And she should have. Damn it, she should have told him about the baby.

TEN MINUTES LATER, Aidan went to the kitchen and found the Summer Island phone book. There weren't any motels or hotels on the island. For the most part, the locals discouraged tourism. But there were a number of bed-and-breakfast places. He dialed Jennifer's number first and was relieved when she answered in person and he didn't get the standard recording.

"Hey Jenn, it's Aidan. I'm here on the island and looking for a place to stay."

"Aidan, you're not kidding? You're really here?"

"I'm on vacation."

"You never take vacations."

"I know. For good reason, apparently." This one sure wasn't going so hot.

"What do you mean?"

"Long story. I'll fill you in later. For now, just please tell me you have room at your B and B. A single bed is all I need. I'm willing to share a bathroom."

"Aidan, it's August." There was mild reproach in Jennifer's voice.

Which meant she didn't have room. And all the other B and B places in town would probably be booked, too. "What about a foldout couch?"

"We have one in the study. And I'd let you stay there, no problem, but that's where we set up the crib."

"Crib? Did someone forget to tell me something?" Was this a new trend? Had every single woman he knew gotten pregnant in the past nine months?

"I'm taking care of my brother's baby while he and his wife are in Argentina. He's teaching a four-week course."

"You're kidding." He knew Jennifer already had to look after her father, who'd suffered a stroke many years ago, and an elderly aunt who'd moved to the island recently. Now she'd taken on her brother's baby, as well?

"Afraid not. Look Aidan, I'm so sorry I can't help you. Where are you now?"

"At Harrison and Justine's."

"They're in Seattle for the month, aren't they? Why don't you just stay there?"

"Because while Harrison gave me a key to the place, Justine also gave a key to Rae Cordell. Rae works for Kincaid Communications, too."

"Do you know each other? The house is certainly big enough for two…."

Not in this case. "I'll figure something out. Not to worry." Aidan heard a squawk. The baby?

"I'm dying to see you, Aidan. Why don't you come for dinner tonight?"

He wanted to see Jennifer, too. But it sounded as though she had her hands full. He didn't want her going to the work of preparing a meal for company. "How about I pick up some sandwiches in town and bring them over?"

"That would be great. I'll make a few

salads to go with them. Do you mind ordering enough for my dad and Aunt Annie, too?"

"No problem."

"And why don't you bring your friend Rae along, as well?"

He hadn't said Rae was a friend. But before he could explain, the baby started squawking again, this time louder than before.

"I've got to go. I'll see you and Rae later, Aidan. I can't wait!"

JENNIFER WAS a naturally kind and hospitable person, so Aidan wasn't surprised she'd extended an invitation to someone she'd never met. That didn't mean he had to pass it on. However, if he didn't, then he'd have to admit to Jennifer that he hadn't, and then she would want to know why.

Aidan decided it would be easier to just invite Rae and let her say no.

He found her in the living room, feet up on the sofa, reading *Forbes*. He told her about the invitation. "Don't feel as if you have to come."

She amazed him by replying calmly, "That was very nice of Jennifer. Yes, I'd love to go."

"You would?"

"Sure." Her eyes betrayed nothing. No hint of the anger from earlier. No angst, no trauma, just…nothing.

"What time do you want to leave?" she asked.

"Half an hour," Aidan said, giving her yet another reason to bow out. Not many women could get ready in that amount of time.

"Fine."

True to her word, Rae was ready within thirty minutes. She'd combed her hair, put on a voluminous sundress and lipstick. She regarded her reflection in the full-length mirror of the foyer despondently. "I look like a puffer fish."

She didn't. She looked beautiful. It choked Aidan to admit it, but it was true. He'd never paid much attention to pregnant women before—he'd never had cause to. But despite her complaints, her insistence that she didn't intend to keep the baby, there was an aura about her.

Rae grabbed her handbag, then waited while Aidan opened the door for her.

"Do you mind if I leave the top down?" he asked, as he helped her into the front seat of his car.

"It's so hot—that would be nice."

She needed a hand sitting down and he guessed she'd need help to get out, as well. He leaned down to find the lever to push the seat back and make more room for her bulk. Inadvertently, his shoulder brushed against her belly. It was surprisingly firm.

He stood up, embarrassed, yet oddly excited by the brief contact. That was his baby in there. And he'd touched her. It was still so incredible to him. Unbelievable and…amazing.

Wanting to touch again, yet knowing he couldn't, he headed for the driver's seat. As he reversed the car out of the driveway, Rae asked, "How far to your friend's house?"

"Lavender Farm is on the north end of the island. About a thirty-minute drive."

They stopped at the Cliffside Diner to pick up the packages of sandwiches that Aidan had ordered, then continued on the main road that circumnavigated the island.

Though paved, the route had many dangerous curves and the posted speed was low. Still, Rae's long hair was whipped by the wind as Aidan accelerated. He leaned over to open the glove compartment and a navy silk scarf fell out.

"Use that."

Rae gave him a questioning look, maybe wondering to whom the scarf belonged, then tied her hair back, as he'd suggested.

As the miles disappeared, Aidan began to relax. It was good to be on Summer Island again. The land to his left broke away to the ocean below with twenty-foot cliffs. The other side of the road was dotted with cultivated farmland and pastures that had been carved from the ancient rain forest. He slowed, in order to pass a small herd of cattle. A portion of the pasture fence had collapsed.

"Aren't they beautiful?" Rae said. "I've never seen such black cows before."

"Those are Kerries, an extremely rare breed of dairy cattle. They don't produce as much milk as a Jersey or a Holstein, but the taste is incredibly creamy."

Rae was surprised by Aidan's detailed

answer. "How do you know so much about cows?"

"For a couple of summers I worked at that farm. Mr. Olsen ran his operation the old-fashioned way, and I milked the cows by hand."

Aidan could still remember the smell of the barn, the feel of the cows' bellies against his head as he crouched low to access the fat, warm teats. There'd been a knack to coaxing the milk out of those teats and he'd been damn proud when he finally heard the satisfying metallic resonance of milk streaming into the galvanized pail held steady between his legs.

"I can't imagine you milking a cow." Rae looked at him speculatively.

"I loved that job. We'd carry the pails into the kitchen and Mrs. Olsen would run the milk through the separator. Once a week she'd give me a bottle of cream to take home to my mother. It was so thick, Mom had to spoon it into her coffee. But boy did it taste great on a bowl of fresh blueberries."

Rae was still looking at him as if he'd just explained that he came from another planet. "Where did you and your mother stay when you were on the island?"

"We used to own the house across from the Kincaid place."

"The pumpkin-colored yoga studio?"

"It was white in those days." Molly Springfield, the new owner, apparently liked bright colors.

From Justine, and Harrison's sister, Nessa, Aidan had heard that the yoga business was thriving, which surprised him. When he'd been a kid, the majority of islanders were fishermen and farmers who resisted the trends and so-called progress of the twentieth century. But they had cell phone service here now, so he supposed a yoga studio had been inevitable.

"Tell me about Jennifer," Rae said. "Have you known her a long time?"

"Pretty much since we were in diapers."

"She's one of Simone DeRosier's original Forget-Me-Not friends, right?"

He grimaced. "You know about that?"

"Last summer that was all anyone at work wanted to talk about. Simone's tragic death and how devastated all of the Forget-Me-Not friends were."

"Yeah, I can imagine." The office grapevine worked well…except where he was concerned, obviously.

"Everyone was shocked when they found out Simone had been murdered. But it was never clear to me why it was assumed to be suicide in the first place."

"Simone was found dead in a running car in her own garage. There was a letter with her that seemed to be a suicide note. It seemed pretty clear-cut at the time."

"So how did Harrison figure out that one of your friends had killed her?"

"There were a number of things that didn't add up. In the end, they all pointed to Emerson." Like Harrison and Gabe, the landscape business owner had been in love with Simone. Only his love had grown into a sick obsession.

"I'm sorry," Rae said. "I shouldn't have raised such a painful topic."

Aidan glanced in the rearview mirror and saw the dark look on his face that must have prompted Rae's apology. He made an effort to smile. "That's okay. It happened a long time ago. Now that Harrison is remarried I think a lot of the wounds have begun to heal."

"Justine is a terrific lady," Rae agreed.

Aidan pointed up the road. "There's Lavender Farm."

He eased off the accelerator. A hand-crafted sign, nailed to the twisted, dark red branch of an arbutus tree, read: Lavender Farm Bed-And-Breakfast.

"Pretty," Rae murmured.

"Wait until you see the rest of the place."

He drove through a grove of tall cedars, veering slowly to the left, and then suddenly they were in a clearing. The two-story clapboard home sat in the midst of a rambling English-style garden. Ivy grew up and along the porch. Delicate blue hydrangea framed the doorway. And flower beds, mostly of lavender, spread out in all directions.

"I feel like I'm in a fairy tale," Rae said, her head swiveling as she took in her surroundings. "Or maybe a nursery rhyme. 'Mary, Mary, quite contrary, how does your garden grow?'"

Taken aback by the prosaic comment, Aidan stared at Rae. When she saw him looking, her smile immediately vanished.

"What?" she demanded. "Did you think I was only capable of appreciating a healthy balance sheet and a profitable operating statement?"

Well, yeah. Up until today, he'd mostly seen Rae in a business environment. Now, all of a sudden, she was pregnant and quoting children's rhymes, and earlier, she'd pulled a loaf of bread from the oven. Okay, that had been out of a package—he'd seen the wrapper on the counter—and she'd burned it so it was inedible, but still, the mere idea that she even knew how to turn on an oven was antithetical to his original view of her.

As Aidan had anticipated, Rae needed help getting out of the front seat. He'd no sooner let go of her hand than he heard his name.

"Aidan!" A woman waved at them from the porch. Jennifer's blond hair was still long and straight—the same as always. Her smile was welcoming. Uncomplicated. The only thing different about this picture was the baby she had balanced on her hip.

"Hey, Jenn." Aidan stepped forward to kiss her cheek. "This is Rae Cordell from our Pittsburgh office. And this must be Erica." He tugged the baby's bare foot gently.

"Hi, Jennifer. It's nice to meet you." Though her words were friendly, Rae didn't seem as relaxed as she'd been on the drive over. Her smile was stiff now, and she hadn't removed her sunglasses, even though they stood in shade.

"Rae, I'm glad you could make it on such short notice." Jennifer shook the other woman's hand, then glanced back at Aidan, her eyes registering surprise.

He should have told her Rae was pregnant.

"We thought we'd eat outside," Jennifer said. "We've set up the picnic table in the back."

"Sounds good. I'll get the food from the car." As Aidan retrieved the paper bags from the backseat, Rae appeared at his side, holding out a hand for one of the sacks.

"You didn't tell me she had a baby," Rae whispered.

"She doesn't—that's her niece. She's babysitting."

With the baby still resting on her hip, Jennifer led her guests to the back garden. It seemed to Aidan that Rae followed almost reluctantly. What was with her? Suddenly she seemed sorry that she'd decided to come. So then, why had she agreed to the invitation? He certainly hadn't pressured her into saying yes.

They reached the patio, where a picnic table had been set with a flowered cloth. Plates and cutlery were stacked next to a pitcher of iced tea.

Sitting side by side at the table were Jennifer's father, Phil, and her aunt Annie. Clearly, the two of them were brother and sister. Both were tall and thin, like Jennifer. However, while Jennifer had fine, feminine features, her aunt's and father's faces were stronger, more angular.

Jennifer provided introductions, then settled the baby in a high chair. Aidan noticed that Rae had elected to sit on the edge of the bench farthest away from the small child. He squeezed himself into the middle, between Rae and Jenn.

"So, dear," Jennifer's father asked as the food was served, "when is your baby due?"

"In about two weeks, is my guess," Annie replied.

"Actually, three," Rae said.

Annie just smiled. "We'll see."

"Until she retired last year, my aunt was a midwife in Prince Rupert," Jennifer explained. "Would you pass the potato salad, please? By the way, Auntie, I used up all our eggs in that salad."

"I'll go to the farm tomorrow and buy more." The older woman passed the salad to her niece. To Rae and Aidan she explained, "Jennifer insists on free-range, organically fed chickens and eggs. That means a trip to the Red Door Farm, which is all the way on the other side of the island."

"Their eggs are the best," Jennifer explained. "How many babies do you think you delivered in your career, Auntie?"

"Oh…hundreds. And I can tell by the way Rae is carrying that she's going to have a—"

"Annie!" Phil admonished. "Maybe Rae wants the sex to be a surprise. What are you hoping for, dear? A boy or a girl?"

Aidan squirmed, uncomfortable on Rae's behalf. She must get these questions all the time. How did she…

"It doesn't matter," Rae said bluntly. "I'm planning to give the child up for adoption."

She twisted to look beyond Aidan to Jennifer. "Can you pass the bowl this way, too, please? I love potato salad."

CHAPTER FOUR

"BUT AIDAN, I don't understand." Jennifer rinsed lingering bubbles from the platter she'd just washed and passed it to him.

"You're not the only one." Aidan dried the china carefully. It was covered with an ornate pattern of gold and flowers and looked about a hundred years old. He knew it was part of a set Jennifer had inherited from her mother. Jenn was always buying replacement pieces on eBay.

"Why would Harrison tell you that you could stay at the summer house if Justine had already given a key to Rae?"

Aidan glanced out the window. Rae and Annie were still seated at the picnic table, talking. Phil had offered to put the baby to bed when Erica had fallen asleep in her high chair.

"I think they were in cahoots," he finally admitted.

Jenn caught on quickly. "You mean they were matchmaking?"

"Yeah." Damn, but he was going to nail Harrison next time he saw him…

"But isn't the timing a little off? I mean, with Rae eight months pregnant and all. Unless… Oh, Aidan. You aren't the father, are you?" She stared at him, oblivious to the fact that she'd left the water running.

He didn't answer, but his face gave him away.

"Well," Jennifer said. "That explains a lot."

He reached over. Turned off the tap. "Yeah, it's quite a mess. I think I'm still in shock. I just found out today that Rae is pregnant."

"How is that possible? I thought you worked together?"

"We *used* to work together. Until I promoted Rae to Pittsburgh."

Jenn draped the washcloth over the edge of the sink. "That's a long way from Seattle."

"That was the idea."

"Oh, Aidan. That's so like you."

"What do you mean?"

"A girl starts to get close, breaks through your defenses…and you banish her to Siberia."

"It was a *promotion*." God, Jenn was as bad as Rae. "What's so bad about Pittsburgh, anyway?"

"This isn't about Pittsburgh. It's about you running away from emotional commitments. You always do, you know."

"That's not fair." But this time, his protest lacked heat. It was true that he preferred to keep his relationships with women tidy. Uncomplicated, mutually beneficial and carefully limited in terms of time.

Nothing about his single night with Rae had fit into any of those categories.

Jenn eyed him with the understanding of someone who'd known him a long time. "So how do you feel about the baby?"

"I don't know. Like I told you, I'm still in shock. Anyway, it doesn't matter how I feel."

"Oh, Aidan. Why would you say that?"

"Given that the baby is being put up for adoption, sperm donor seems more descriptive of my role."

"You sound a little bitter about that. Do you want Rae to keep the baby?"

"God, no." Of course, he didn't. The route Rae had chosen was best for all of them in the long run. It was just that he needed time to come to grips with the idea.

"That's something else I can't understand," Jennifer said. "Rae sounded so matter-of-fact when she said she was giving up the baby for adoption. As if the baby were no more important to her than an out-of-date piece of furniture."

She *had* sounded a little callous, but Aidan felt compelled to defend her. "Rae's pretty serious about her career. A family was never part of her plan."

Jennifer eyed a picture of Erica that was displayed on the fridge. "Yes, well, plans change. Life happens and people adjust. Maybe you and Rae should at least consider…"

"Oh, no. We're not considering anything."

"But—"

"Please, Jenn. It's bad enough that Harrison and Justine have tricked us into staying at the same house. Don't you turn on me, too."

As he'd expected, Jenn was too softhearted to press her point of view any further. "Of course, I'll support whatever decision you make. You're one of my oldest friends, Aidan. I can't tell you how great it is to see you again."

He gave her a hug. "It's good to be here."

Surprisingly, it was. Not everything on this island had been soured by Simone, and that was a good thing to remind himself of now and then.

"How are things with you?" he asked, pulling back from the friendly embrace.

"I've been getting more serious about the lavender. I'm not just making sachets now, but linen water, bath oils and I'm developing a new hand cream, too."

"You were always the crafty one in the group. Say, how are Nessa and Gabe doing? Harrison told me their divorce was just finalized. He's pretty worried about his little sister."

"Nessa is doing well. Her MS has been in remission for quite a while now."

"I'm relieved to hear that." He still couldn't believe Nessa had had the misfortune to contract such a serious disease.

"Yes. And the day care she opened last

September keeps her busy and happy, though I'm glad she closes for the summer and takes a nice, long break. Of course, right now Autumn's staying with her."

Aidan remembered Harrison telling him that Autumn didn't want to leave the island during the summer, and that she'd convinced her father to let her stay with her aunt for a couple of weeks. Aidan was pretty sure Harrison and Justine were making the most of the opportunity for a second honeymoon. They'd been married less than a year, after all.

"I'm glad Nessa's doing so well. What about Gabe?"

"He's struggling," Jenn admitted. "Gabe took the divorce really hard. Which is surprising, considering how he treated Nessa when she was his wife."

"No kidding." Even after Simone's marriage to Harrison, and his own marriage to Nessa, Gabe had never stopped carrying a torch for the singer. And she'd taken full advantage of his feelings for her. Whenever Harrison was working late or on a business trip, she'd gone crying to Gabe. Apparently,

Gabe had thought nothing of ignoring his wife so he could cater to Simone's emotional needs.

"I'd like to see Nessa before I leave."

Jennifer looked puzzled. "I'm sure that won't be a problem. You're here for three weeks, right?"

"That was the idea. Before I found out who I'd be boarding with." He glanced out the window again. Rae was holding back her thick hair with both hands, resting her elbows on the picnic table. Whatever Jennifer's aunt was saying, it seemed to have the younger woman fascinated. "What do you think they're talking about?"

Jennifer followed his gaze. Shrugged. "Babies, probably."

He felt a nervous twitch of his stomach. Babies, indeed. And he'd thought he was stressed out in Seattle.

"YOU WORRIED ABOUT having this baby?"

Annie's watery eyes were almost the same color as the lavender blossoms in the garden behind her. Rae still couldn't get over how pretty this place was. The house, the gardens, even the picnic table, which had been set with real china and not the cheap outdoor plastic stuff Rae used when she had a barbecue.

Which had been once, come to think of it.

"I'm scared shitless, Annie." She cupped her hands over her enormous belly. "You'd think we humans would have evolved past this point by now. I mean, there's got to be an easier way."

Annie seemed amused by that. "Such as?"

"Test tubes and incubators, maybe? I don't know—I'm not a doctor. I just think our current system is a little archaic." She gazed skyward. "No offense, God. I'm sure you did the best you could at the time."

"Rae!"

Had she shocked Jennifer's aunt? No, Annie looked more amused than scandalized. Rae leaned forward over the picnic table. "There've been a lot of scientific advancements since Adam and Eve. You know what I mean?"

Annie was laughing now. "Forty-five years of midwifery and I've never met a first-time mother quite like you."

Rae could believe that. Most women like her would be smart enough to make sure they didn't get pregnant in the first place. She'd never been the kind of girl who dreamed about her wedding day or thought about names for the children she would have one day.

She read *BusinessWeek* and *Forbes,* not *Wedding Bells* or *Today's Parent.*

And she was scared as hell of delivering this baby.

"Well, stop worrying," Annie said. "You may not think you want children, but you have a body built for popping them out."

"You can tell?" Rae looked down. She could remember what her figure *used* to look like, but right now, as far as she was concerned, she resembled nothing more than a blob.

"I've delivered hundreds of babies. Of course, I can tell."

"Hundreds of babies? Tell me, Annie. Did you ever lose a mother?"

Annie was so animated that she hadn't seemed at all old to Rae until that moment. As the spark left her eyes, she folded her weathered, wrinkled hands on the picnic table.

"Once. I lost a mother once."

Rae felt her stomach tighten ominously. She knew she shouldn't ask, but like a teenage girl drawn to a horror movie, she had to know. "What happened?"

"I worked in a rural area, you have to understand. We referred all the high-risk cases to Prince Rupert, sometimes even to Vancouver. But there was this one woman. Lila was her name. She was as high-risk as they come. A smoker, a drinker and diabetic, too. As if that wasn't enough, when she was thirty-eight weeks along, her baby shifted into breech position and wouldn't budge."

"That doesn't sound good."

"It wasn't. We told Lila's husband to take her to the city. We arranged an appointment with a specialist. But they wouldn't go."

"Did the baby survive?"

Annie shook her head. "We lost them both. Full moon that night. I'll never forget how the father cried."

"That must have been terrible."

"The worst night of my life. And I've seen a lot of hard things."

Rae could only imagine. As a midwife,

Annie had dealt with life at its most elemental level. So different from the business world that Rae had chosen. What would Annie make of that world? The modern office buildings and posh conference rooms? The wheeling and dealing over morning lattes and evening cocktails?

"Maybe I shouldn't have told you about Lila, when you're already worried about your own delivery. But you'll be seeing Dr. Marshall, right?"

Rae nodded. "Justine set up weekly appointments on my behalf before I arrived."

"Dr. Marshall's a little young, but she knows what she's doing."

Despite her nerves, Rae had to smile. A little young? She'd had her first appointment with the doctor last week, and the physician was in her late forties, possibly even fifty.

"You're going to be fine, Rae." Annie patted her hand.

Rae wanted to believe her. She seemed like a straight shooter, this Annie, and Rae liked her. But all Rae's instincts warned her that she wasn't going to be fine.

Something was going to go wrong. She

didn't know what. She just knew it. Which was strange, because she wasn't usually the type to indulge in premonitions.

She noticed Annie eyeing her speculatively. "I suppose you think I'm a freak because I don't want to keep this baby?"

"Well…if a woman isn't cut out to be a mother, it's better that she has the courage to admit it up front. I've delivered plenty of babies to families that weren't fit to raise them. Alcoholic mothers. Abusive fathers." Annie's eyes became still more glazed, as she thought back to the past. "Just about broke my heart to pass those little bundles to those parents. In fact, one time I didn't. Got into a little trouble with the law over that."

"What kind of trouble?"

"Never mind, hon. It all worked out in the end. I finally persuaded the powers that be that the child's needs had to come first."

"Well, I'm not an alcoholic and I'd like to think I'm not abusive, either." Though her personal assistant at work might disagree with that second point. "But there are other ways of being an unfit mother."

"Sure there are."

"A child knows when she isn't wanted. That kind of emotional abuse is just as bad as getting used as a punching bag, don't you think?"

Now Annie's eyes were suddenly sharp. And focused on her.

Rae realized she needed to cover her tracks. "I mean, that's what *I* think. But you're the expert. I'd like to know your opinion."

"Being loved is the most important thing. You're absolutely right about that."

"Exactly. And some women just don't have the maternal makeup to deal with a crying baby or a snotty-nosed toddler." Or a chubby, school-age child who turned into a gangly, awkward adolescent.

"Some women don't." Annie's tone was completely nonjudgmental.

"Did you have children, Annie?"

"No. Funny, isn't it? I was too busy helping other women delivering babies to have any of my own. Never met the right man to have them with. Most wanted me to give up my career and I would never do that."

"Me, either."

Annie reached across the table to pat her

hand. "My career provided me with a very full and satisfying life. Are you sure that yours will be enough for you?"

"Of course it will. Before I found out I was pregnant, I was very happy." Okay, "happy" might be a bit of an exaggeration.

Once, before she'd met Aidan, she'd been close to happy. Satisfied, actually. Her mother's death had released her from a lifetime of guilt and melancholy, and her career had been taking off. As for men, she'd dated occasionally, but she'd felt no emotional connection to any of them.

She assumed the flaw was hers. She had something missing in her, emotionally. Given her childhood, that wasn't surprising.

But then she'd met Aidan, and for the first time in her life she'd experienced it all: emotional ups and downs, the thrill of seeing him walk into the room and dizzy joy when he actually smiled at her. Suddenly, all the romantic songs she heard on the radio made sense to her. She had rented a DVD of *The Way We Were* and actually cried.

"It's your life, Rae. Just make sure that you focus on the things that are important to you." Annie's attention shifted back to the farmhouse. "Aidan is waving at us. I think it's time for you to go."

Rae looked over her shoulder. Sure enough, there was Aidan, walking with Jennifer by his side. They looked so relaxed and easy together.

What would it be like to have a friend like that? A friend you'd known forever, someone you could really talk to?

As a child, she hadn't been good at making friends. The closest she'd come was the next-door neighbor. Effie had been gray-haired and plump. She had a large extended family in Greece, but she'd lived alone since her children had grown up and her husband had died. She'd seemed to enjoy Rae's visits.

Rae would drop over for a piece of honey-soaked baklava, or one of the sugar-coated *kourabiedes* Effie baked for Christmas, and Effie would talk. Effie always had something to say, usually anecdotes about her childhood in Greece, and Rae would sit and listen, feeling wonderfully safe and warm.

Yes, those afternoons she had felt happy.

But when Rae was sixteen, Effie had

decided to move back to Greece. Her house was sold to a family with three young children; a couple of times the mother asked Rae to babysit, but she always claimed to have too much homework.

"Ready to head home?" Aidan asked.

She nodded, then sighed and untangled her bulk from the picnic bench. Once she was standing, she held out a hand to Jennifer's aunt.

"It was really interesting talking to you, Annie."

Annie took hold of her hand as if she didn't intend to let go. "I have more stories to tell you. And cream for your belly. You come back and see me soon."

"I will," Rae promised. To her surprise, she really wanted to.

AT TWO IN THE MORNING, Rae woke up. She needed to pee. This was getting old, not sleeping through the night.

And the floor was cold. Where were her slippers? Her housecoat was on the chair where she'd left it, but the slippers were missing in action.

Rae opened her door and headed down the

hall. A night-light had been plugged into one of the wall sockets, probably for Autumn's benefit, but Rae was grateful for it, too.

From the far end of the hall, a line of light glowed beneath the door to Aidan's room.

Why was he up at this hour?

Probably he couldn't fall asleep. Rae could understand. When she'd found out she was pregnant, she hadn't slept at all for several nights. It wasn't her fault that Aidan had discovered the news so late, and Rae refused to feel guilty about it. If Aidan hadn't deliberately isolated himself from her, he *would* have known.

She slipped into the bathroom, took care of business, then headed back to her room. She'd almost made it, too, when Aidan's door opened.

He was still wearing the jeans and shirt he'd had on earlier in the evening.

"Having trouble sleeping?" he asked her.

"That last glass of water was a big mistake." She tightened the sash on her bathrobe. Which was another mistake, since she only ended up emphasizing the roundness of her stomach. She saw Aidan's gaze go there. Linger there.

Hey, buddy. I have a face.

"What about you?" she asked, grudgingly. "Need a sleeping pill?" She couldn't use them in her condition, but she had them in the travel bag she always took on business trips.

"I'll pass. One sleepless night won't kill me."

Despite her determination to stay tough, she felt a twinge of sympathy for him. "You've had a bit of a shock."

"I'll say."

She waited for him to upbraid her again, for not sharing the news sooner. And if he even tried, she was more than prepared to fight back.

But in his eyes she saw more resignation than outrage.

"So," she said. "Will you be leaving in the morning?" On the drive home he'd made it clear that he wouldn't be staying any longer than necessary.

"That's what I've been thinking about."

He leaned a hand on the door frame and

she tried not to notice how good he looked. He skied to stay in shape—skied and mountain biked. Clearly his regimen worked, because he had not gained an ounce since their night together in Philadelphia.

It wasn't fair. If babies couldn't be produced simply with test tubes and incubators, couldn't the process at least require the man to gain weight, too?

"So," she prodded. "The results of all this thinking are…?"

"For eight months you've been dealing with this—" he cleared his throat "—this pregnancy, on your own."

"True."

"It's time I did my share."

"Great." She cupped her hands around her belly. "I'll just slip this off and hand it over."

His grin was the first sign she'd been given that he still had a sense of humor.

"I'll bet you wish you could."

"You have no idea."

He realized she'd been leaning against the wall. "I'm sorry. I'm keeping you up, and you're obviously exhausted."

But she wanted to hear what he had to say.

How he was planning to start shouldering his share of the load. "It's okay. I'm going to have to pee in another hour, anyway. It's hardly worth going back to bed."

He didn't buy it. "Come on, Rae." He opened her bedroom door and waited at the doorway until she'd settled back into bed.

"Can I get you anything?"

"Yeah, a pedicure and a box of bonbons."

He didn't laugh as she'd expected him to. "Maybe tomorrow."

"But tomorrow you'll be gone."

"Is that what you want?"

The man was infuriating. It was too late for mind games. "I told you there was plenty of room in this house for two. You're the one who decided you didn't want to stay."

There'd been a split second when she'd first seen him in the kitchen, when she'd had a crazy thought. *He's come for me,* her foolish self had cheered. *He's finally realized how much he loves me, and he's come to get me and take me home.*

It hurt to admit to herself just how pathetic she could be. Her only consolation was that

Aidan didn't know about this weakness of hers. Her weakness for him.

And that was what really made her crazy. Even now that she knew he was the sort of man who would sleep with an employee, then move her like a pawn to a different city, she was still deeply affected by him.

She hated that.

Thank God he was leaving.

"So where are you going?" she asked again.

"I've decided I'd like to stay. If that's still okay with you."

Why the about-face? She tried to read the answer in his eyes, but it was too late and she was too tired. "I don't understand."

"It's not that complicated. I'd like to stay here with you until the baby's born."

Rae's stomach dropped at the word *baby*. "Aidan, I've already told you that you don't have to worry about that. It's nothing to do with you."

"You're wrong. This baby definitely has something to do with me. And for the next few weeks, so do you."

CHAPTER FIVE

"GO TO HELL, AIDAN. I didn't need you for the first eight months of this pregnancy and I don't need you now."

Aidan took Rae's insult without comment.

"If I were you," she continued, "I'd catch a flight to Hawaii and enjoy myself. Have yourself a real vacation."

"Oh, really. You want me to sit on a beach and drink mai tais while you stay here and have our baby?"

"Don't call it 'ours.' It isn't *ours*, Aidan. It belongs to Julia and Neil Thompson. *They're* the ones who'll get to call this baby 'ours.'"

Aidan reeled. "Julia and Neil Thompson?"

She nodded. "I arranged the adoption through an agency. I handpicked the parents myself, and they're perfect. Julia's a kindergarten teacher. She's got to love kids, right?

And Neil's a social worker, so he'll be one of those warm, sensitive types, too."

"Warm and sensitive."

Every time Rae stopped talking it seemed all Aidan could do was repeat the last few words she'd said.

"Snap out of it, Aidan. What's the problem? I told you I was putting the baby up for adoption."

"But…" Aidan blinked his eyes several times. "Do you have more information on these people?"

"Sure. The agency sent me reams of background information."

"Okay." He took a deep breath. "You're tired. You should get some sleep. But in the morning I'm going to want to read everything you've got."

"But…"

He shut the door and she heard his footsteps as he walked away down the hall.

Oddly enough, Rae did fall asleep after that, and when she woke up the next morning, Aidan's words were still in her head. *This baby definitely has something to do to me. And for the next few weeks, so do you.*

He'd made his decision out of guilt and responsibility. Rae was certain this was the case. And yet, she had to admit that she was glad, really, really glad, he'd decided to stay.

She wasn't happy about feeling this way. In fact, she hated to think that the man still held this much power over her.

But there it was. When it came to Aidan Wythe, she was an absolute fool.

Of course, there was always the possibility that he'd rethought his position over the past couple of hours. For all she knew, he could have tossed his suitcase back in his car and taken the first ferry off the island this morning.

Rae dressed for her morning walk in shorts and T-shirt, then headed to the kitchen for breakfast. In the past, this was a meal she had always skipped, but since she'd found out she was pregnant, she'd become more disciplined.

The sight of Aidan standing by the stove stopped her short. "You're still here?"

"I told you last night I was staying."

"Yes. But before you slept with me, you promised I was going to be the head of the acquisitions department. Then, instead, you made me head of operations in Pittsburgh." She perched on a bar stool. "I just thought you might have changed your mind again."

Aidan gave her a dirty look, but instead of defending himself, he pointed at a frying pan on top of the gas range. Now she noticed a pitcher of beaten eggs, and bowls of diced peppers, mushrooms and ham on the side.

"Would you like an omelet?"

How could she say no?

When they were done eating, Aidan asked to see the information on the adoptive parents. Rae brought down the envelope from her bedroom, but Aidan didn't even glance inside.

"What are you going to do now?" he asked.

"Walk to the beach."

"Sounds good."

"It does?"

"Yeah." He shot her a challenging look. "Do you mind if I come with you?"

What was with him? He couldn't *want* to be spending all this time with her. Yet, he seemed perfectly content as he donned his sunglasses and locked the front door on the way out.

There were no sidewalks, so they kept to the left-hand side of the road.

"Why did your mother choose this island for a vacation spot? Why not someplace in the U.S.?"

"She and Harrison's mother were best friends. And the Kincaids have had a place here since the eighteen hundreds."

"Is the house that old?"

"It's been renovated several times, but I believe the Kincaids have always been faithful to the original architecture."

Aidan filled her in on bits and pieces of Summer Island's history. As they neared the beach, he shielded his eyes from the sun and focused on someone ahead of them. "That looks like Harrison's sister. She has Autumn with her."

It was early in the day and there weren't many people on the beach, just a few mothers with young children. Rae had no trouble spotting the woman Aidan was talking about. Nessa was a petite, pretty woman with dark hair. She was tossing a Frisbee to a little girl who appeared to be around seven years old. The little girl had dark hair, too, but she was more than just pretty. Even at her young age, Rae could tell she was going to grow up to be exceptionally beautiful.

Clearly, this was Simone DeRosier's daughter. Though the jazz singer had been dead for a year by the time Rae joined Kincaid Communications, she had heard plenty of stories about the famous woman from her coworkers. According to the rumors, though Simone had often been away on tours and promotional gigs, she'd been a devoted mother, if not quite a devoted wife.

"I heard that Harrison's sister has multiple sclerosis," Rae said. "But she looks perfectly normal."

"We're hoping she's going to be one of the lucky ones," Aidan said. "The disease has been in remission for almost a year now."

"Autumn is beautiful," Rae said. "She looks amazingly like her mother."

"Yeah. That's what everyone says."

Aidan sounded gloomy, and Rae shot him a curious look. Simone DeRosier had been a classic beauty. Surely the fact that her daughter resembled her was not a bad thing?

NESSA KINCAID BROOKE spun the Frisbee toward her niece, then froze as a pregnant woman approached the beach from the road. Nessa had antennae for expectant mothers, just as in a crowd she always picked out babies…especially infants.

The pregnant woman walked in that particular wide-footed way that was so common to the final trimester. One hand rested on her rounded belly.

What would it feel like to have a baby inside you? With all her heart, Nessa envied the woman. She was beautiful, too, with dark, wavy hair and a fair, yet rosy complexion.

Nessa checked out the man beside her, then blinked as she recognized Aidan.

Harrison had told her Aidan was coming to the island for a holiday. So that meant this woman with him was Rae Cordell, the up-and-coming corporate genius Harrison was so pumped about.

He and Justine had told her that, while Aidan wasn't saying anything, the scuttlebutt at Kincaid Communications was that

Rae and Aidan had had an affair, then Aidan had transferred Rae to the Pittsburgh office.

It all sounded too sordid to Nessa. Not like Aidan, at all. Yet, the fact that he was here with Rae now, made it likely the story was true.

"Watch out, Auntie Nessa!"

The Frisbee was coming right for her head. Nessa snatched it out of the air, then laughed at Autumn. "That was a good throw." She pointed to Aidan. "But look who's here."

Autumn glanced over her shoulder, then started to run. "Uncle Aidan!"

Nessa followed at a slower pace, watching as Autumn hurled herself into Aidan's arms for a hug. Aidan's eyes were on Nessa as he squeezed the little girl briefly, then gently set her on the ground.

In the past, Nessa had noticed a certain reserve in Aidan's manner with the little girl. Given the close relationship between Aidan and the Kincaid family—in particular, Harrison—that had always struck her as odd.

"Aidan, hi. Harrison told me you were coming to the island."

"Hey, Nessa. It's good to see you. You're looking terrific." He hugged her warmly.

"Uncle Aidan!" Autumn tugged on the hem of his T-shirt. "Auntie Nessa taught me some new songs. Do you want to hear them?"

He brushed his curly hair back from his forehead. "Umm…"

"Later, honey!" Nessa laughed. "Give us a minute to chat, first." She held out a hand to Rae, trying not to look too longingly at the obvious evidence of her pregnancy. "Hi, I've been meaning to drop by the summer-house to introduce myself. Harrison has told me how invaluable you are at Kincaid Communications."

"Invaluable?" She glanced at Aidan. "I'm glad to hear *someone* thinks so."

He winced, but said nothing.

Hmm, so what was going on here?

"Anyway, thank you, Nessa," Rae continued. "It's nice to meet you, too. Your niece sure is the spitting image of her mother, isn't she?"

"Autumn's a doll, all around."

"Can I make a sand castle?" Autumn

asked, clearly not affected by the compliment, which was probably a good thing.

"Go right ahead. The sand toys are in the bag by our beach towels." As soon as Nessa pointed them out, Autumn was off and running.

"So how are you feeling, Nessa?" Aidan dropped an arm around her shoulders and looked at her with genuine concern.

She knew he was wondering about the MS. She'd been diagnosed last summer. It had been a terrible shock, yet in an odd way she was glad it had happened. Knowing she had an unpredictable disease that had the potential to cripple her, or worse, she'd come to understand better that her time was limited…and precious.

Finally, she'd found the strength to end an unsatisfying marriage and follow her passion.

"I'm well, Aidan. My business closes for the summer, but I'm looking forward to starting up again in September."

"Oh? What's your business?" Rae asked. "Are you a corporate genius like your brother?"

"Hardly." Nessa laughed. "I run the Sandy Hill Day Care."

"Oh."

Rae clearly wasn't impressed, but that didn't diminish Nessa's own pride in her new enterprise. "I'm a teacher by training, but I really prefer working with younger children. Day care is perfect. And I love having summers off to spend lots of time with my niece."

Her heart warmed as she watched Autumn scooping up mounds of coarse sand and shaping them into a castlelike shape. Autumn was such a dear girl and it was so good to see her happy after the trauma of losing her mother.

She turned back to Rae, who pretty clearly had no interest in maternal matters. Nessa wondered what kind of mother she was going to be to the baby she was carrying. Would she hire a nanny and go back to work at six weeks, or something crazy like that?

"Jenn tells me your divorce is final," Aidan said.

Nessa experienced a familiar, yet fading, sadness. "Yes. It's depressing in one way, but it was time for both of us to look for happiness elsewhere." She turned her rueful gaze toward Rae. "We never managed to bring out the best in each other."

"Simone didn't help matters," Aidan said gruffly.

He'd always blamed Simone. Not just for the failure of Nessa's marriage, but also for not being a better wife to Harrison. Once they'd shared this bitter attitude, but during the past year Nessa had finally let go of the resentment.

"Simone could be selfish. But she could be incredibly generous at times, too. Remember all those trips she took Jennifer on?" Nessa pointed out, determined to be fair. "She was a good mother. And in their own way, she and Harrison were happy together."

"You can't tell me you don't blame her at all anymore?" Aidan said.

"Not really. Honestly." She touched his arm, wishing he could let go of some of his own anger. Aidan always felt things so deeply.

Even as a little boy, he'd been that way. She remembered his abiding attachment to a set of Hot Wheels cars. She'd been thrilled when he let her play with them, but he'd always hung around, watching to make sure she didn't lose any.

"Well, look at that." Rae nodded at a vehicle as it pulled into the beach parking area. "That's the first cop car I've seen since I've been here. Do you think there's been a call about a suspected littering?"

Nessa looked eagerly toward the road. She'd been wondering if Dex would see her car in the parking lot and stop during his routine morning round of the island.

Sure enough, it was Dex who stepped out of the driver's seat. He waved, and she smiled back. She was always so glad to see him. If circumstances had been different, they'd probably be dating by now. But she considered herself lucky enough to call him a good friend.

AIDAN COULDN'T BELIEVE Nessa was so forgiving of Simone. There was no doubt in his mind that the singer was responsible for Nessa and Gabe's divorce.

Simone was dead. But the damage she'd inflicted on the people she'd claimed to love lived on.

He wondered if any of the "Forget-Me-Not" friends ever wondered how their lives would have turned out if Simone's father had never brought her to the island. Nessa was too young to be an official member of the group, but Gabe had been the very heart of the gang.

If he hadn't had Simone to pine over, would he have made a success of his marriage to Nessa?

"You know this guy?" Rae asked, looking from the police officer to Nessa.

Nessa didn't seem to hear, she was too focused on Dex's approach. Were those stars in her eyes? Aidan had heard Harrison speculate on the nature of the friendship between these two. From what Aidan could see, Dex was just as enthralled with Nessa as she was with him.

Well, that was good. Nessa deserved a little happiness after all she'd been through. "Hey, Dex," he said, as the other man joined their group.

Dex tore his gaze from Nessa long enough to nod at him. "Aidan. Heard you were back." He extended a hand toward Rae. "I'm Dex Ulrich."

"He's in charge of the local RCMP detachment," Aidan elaborated. The last time Aidan had talked to Dex had been a year ago, after the drama of discovering the truth behind Simone's death. Emerson's subsequent suicide had closed the affair and now everyone involved had had a year to recover.

Seemed like the past twelve months had been good to Dex. He looked as if he'd dropped a few pounds. And there was definitely a spring to his step that hadn't been there before.

The four of them made polite conversation for a few minutes, but it soon became evident that the person Dex really wanted to talk to was Nessa.

Rae quickly picked up on those vibes, and began drifting toward the water. She kicked off her sandals and waded up to her ankles. Aidan followed her.

"This is a nice community. I can see why you and Harrison are so fond of it."

"Yeah, it's a good place, with mostly good people. So what do you make of Dex? Do you think he has his eye on Harrison's sister?"

"Absolutely." A wave rolled in, up to Rae's

calves. She took several steps backward and bumped into a little boy.

"Oh, sorry!" She caught him before he fell. "Are you okay?"

The towheaded child, a little younger than Autumn and very skinny, rubbed his hands over his clothes. "I didn't get wet, did I?"

"No." Aidan wondered why it mattered. They were on the beach, after all, and it was an extremely warm day.

"My legs did. Now they'll get muddy."

"I'm sorry," Rae apologized again, though she was clearly as confused as Aidan about why the boy was upset.

"We have a blanket," Aidan said. "How about I dry you off?"

The clear relief on the boy's face gave him his answer. He scooped the small child up onto his shoulders and headed for the beach bag Rae had dropped a few yards behind them.

On the way, they passed Nessa and Dex— who were still deep in conversation. Nessa stopped whatever she was saying and gave the small boy a friendly smile.

"Hi, Tyler. I see you've met my friends." To Aidan and Rae, she explained, "Tyler comes to my day care before and after school. He's a really great guy. Tyler, this is Aidan Wythe and Rae Cordell."

"Hi, Nessa," Tyler said, cheerfully. "We're going to dry my legs."

"When you're done, I'll introduce you to my niece," Nessa offered. "She's about your age. Maybe you can play together." She returned to her conversation with Dex, and Aidan continued up the beach. Rae beat him to the bag and hastily pulled out a plaid car blanket, spreading it over the tiny pebbles that passed for sand in this cove.

He shifted the boy to the blanket, then patted the water off his skinny legs. "Where's your mom, Tyler?" Aidan scanned the beach, looking for a worried mother.

"She's dead," Tyler said quietly.

Oh, man. "Are you with your dad? Or a babysitter?"

Tyler shook his head to both questions, as he plopped down in the center of the blanket.

"You mean you're here on your own?"

Tyler nodded.

That didn't seem right. The boy couldn't be more than six years old. "I used to play here all the time when I was little," Aidan said. Only never alone.

"Yeah? What did you do?"

Aidan thought back to when he'd been that small and listed some of the games he'd played.

"Who'd you play with?"

"I had four good friends. Jennifer, Emerson, Gabe and Harrison—he's Nessa's older brother."

"Nessa's nice. She *never* yells."

Aidan and Rae exchanged a glance and a frown. Something definitely wasn't right here. For one thing, the child was very skinny. "Are you hungry, Tyler?" He'd seen Rae shove some snacks inside that beach bag of hers.

Rae picked up on his suggestion. "Would you like an apple or an oatmeal cookie?"

Predictably, the boy said, "Cookie." As he reached out, Aidan noticed bruises on his wrist. He glanced over at Rae and saw her frowning again.

She'd seen the marks, too.

Aidan sat next to the boy. "Why can't you get dirty, Tyler?" he asked.

Rae held her breath waiting for Tyler's answer. She didn't like the look of those bruises and she could tell Aidan didn't, either. Besides, though she knew nothing about kids, even she could figure out that Tyler was too young to be wandering around the edge of an ocean without supervision.

Tyler had gobbled up his cookie, and now she gave him another one. "Do you like being clean, Tyler?" she asked.

He shrugged, keeping his eyes on the cookie. "My dad doesn't like doing laundry," he mumbled.

"So, where is your dad right now, buddy?" Aidan brushed a hand gently over the small boy's blond hair.

He should be wearing a hat, too, Rae realized, with hair that fair. And sunscreen, though he was so deeply tanned it was clear he'd gone the summer without any such protection.

"At home. He got fired, again."

"That's too bad." Rae dug into her bag and came up with a juice box. She handed it to the boy.

"Gosh, thanks!" With awkward little

fingers, he tore the wrapper off the straw, then poked it into the box. For several seconds he drank noisily.

When Tyler was finished, Aidan asked, "Want us to walk you home?"

The boy's eyes grew wary. "No, thanks. I have to go now." He scrambled off the blanket and raced along the beach without a backward glance. A moment later, Nessa was introducing him to Autumn. The little girl passed him one of her pails and he wandered up the beach and began collecting sea shells, presumably for the castle.

Rae caught Nessa's eye. She and the cop had been watching the young boy, too. Nessa gave Rae a shrug that seemed to say, "I don't like it, either, but there's not much we can do."

"Something's wrong." Aidan still monitored the boy, as well. "I should have a talk with his father."

"Maybe you should." Discreetly, she studied Aidan's attentive expression. Earlier, when she'd seen how awkward he was with Autumn, she'd assumed that Aidan maybe wasn't all that good around kids. But he'd easily established a rapport with Tyler, so that couldn't be the case.

Rae didn't think it was the fact that Autumn was a girl that made Aidan uncomfortable. At work, he had no trouble working with and relating well to his female employees. Plus he clearly had excellent relationships with Jennifer and Nessa.

No, there was something that made him uncomfortable with Autumn in particular. But Rae couldn't imagine what that might be.

CHAPTER SIX

AFTER HE'D FINISHED making a sand castle with Autumn, Tyler came back to their blanket for another snack. This time Aidan gave him an apple, wishing he had something more substantial, like a burger, to offer.

"I think I should call your dad," Aidan said, when the boy was done. He pulled his cell phone out of his back pocket. "Do you know your phone number, Tyler?"

"No." Tyler's eyes turned wary. "I gotta go play."

"Maybe Nessa knows his number," Rae suggested.

"Good idea. I'll go ask her." She and Autumn were back to playing Frisbee on the grass. He wandered over, but it was no use.

"The number's programmed in on my cell phone, but I didn't bring it with me."

"Okay. Well, I'll just…" Aidan scanned the area for Tyler, but couldn't see him. "Where did he go?"

Nessa looked around, as well. "Maybe he decided to walk home after all. It's sad, but he runs around on his own all the time."

Aidan returned to Rae, who'd begun packing their things back into her bag. He noticed her cheeks had turned rosy, despite the hat she was wearing.

"Are you going to be okay walking in this heat?" Aidan figured the temperature was in the eighties now. Plus, the breeze had died down.

"I'll be fine."

Aidan shook the crumbs off the blanket, then folded it, while Rae retrieved her sandals and worked them back onto her feet. While she was preoccupied, he stole a long look at her.

Rae, pregnant, was still a shock to his senses.

The Rae he remembered, the Rae he'd met in Seattle about a year ago, had been an executive, a professional woman at the beginning of what would obviously be a brilliant professional career. Rae was intelligent and ambitious, with great business instincts and tenacious negotiating skills.

In the four months they'd worked together, he'd never once heard her talk about any of the subjects the other women he knew routinely discussed among themselves. If decorating, fashion, cooking or relationships held any interest to Rae Cordell, she'd never let on.

Like him, she seemed to think business 24-7.

And now she was pregnant. He glanced at her belly, again overwhelmed by the urge to touch it.

A baby was inside there. A baby who still seemed surreal to him, even though to Rae the baby was an inescapable reality.

How trapped she must feel. If he chose, he could return to Seattle and pretend this little problem of his didn't exist. But Rae couldn't do that.

Which was why he couldn't, either.

He stuffed the blanket into the bag, then shouldered it. "You're sure you're okay? I could run back for my car."

"I'm pregnant. Not an invalid."

Okay. He'd tried to be considerate. But clearly Rae wasn't going to make it easy for him. He fell into step beside her, letting her set the pace, which was faster than he'd expected.

She gathered her hair off her neck, fastened it with an elastic, and all without breaking stride. "That kid, Tyler—you were good with him."

"I was?"

"Didn't you see the way he looked at you, Aidan? Like you were some kind of god. He kept coming back to talk to you."

"He wanted cookies."

"The cookies were just an excuse. He liked you." She gave him a speculative look, as if she was trying to understand why.

"He liked you, too."

"Hardly." She tossed her head back. "I've always been terrible with children."

"Been around a lot of kids, have you?"

"Well…no."

"Then how do you figure you're not good with them? Maybe it's an acquired skill. Like applied economics."

"Applied economics is logical. Children

aren't. It's like the ability to carry a tune. You're either born with the ability or you're not."

"Is this your way of convincing me that you're doing the right thing by giving up our baby?"

She glowered at him. "I've told you not to call it that. Anyway, I don't need to convince you of *anything*. I'm not looking for your approval."

"Yeah, I kind of noticed that. Asking for my approval would have involved telling me about the baby. By the way, were you *ever* going to say anything?"

"Don't pull that guilt trip on me. You would have known if you'd bothered to check up on the Pittsburgh office just once in the past three months."

"That's pretty lame, Rae."

She glowered again, and he wondered if it was anger that was putting that red flush on her cheeks—or heatstroke. Damn it, he should have insisted on going back for the car.

"When I said there was room for both of us in the house, I wasn't planning on you arguing with me the whole time."

Him arguing? What about her? He bit back an explosive reply. She was the one who'd been pregnant for the past eight months. He supposed she had a right to be a little testy.

Besides, he didn't really want to open up a debate on what she should do with the baby. Giving it up for adoption was the logical, responsible solution to a difficult dilemma.

"Sorry." The apology was difficult, but he forced himself to go further. "For the record, I happen to agree with your decision to go the adoption route."

"Great. That's just peachy, Aidan."

Why was she still so angry? He'd said he was sorry and that he agreed with her. Rae used to be so reasonable. Was it pregnancy that did this to a woman?

At last they were within sight of the summerhouse. "When do you see the doctor next?"

"One o'clock, tomorrow. Why would you care?" Her lower jaw dropped a little. "You're not…"

"Coming? Of course, I am. As little as it apparently means to you, I am the father. And I intend to start pulling my weight. Remember?"

THE NEXT DAY, Rae slipped out of the house early so she could walk to the beach on her own. Aidan had been so attentive the previous day that she'd been left feeling overwhelmed. She needed some distance, to put the situation into perspective.

She trod the familiar road, trying not to compare this outing to yesterday's. Being with Aidan tended to make everything a little more interesting. But she couldn't let herself become used to having him around. She needed to remember that his concern wasn't motivated by any special feelings for her. Guilt, pure and simple, was why he was here.

And when this was over, he'd feel he'd done his duty. She'd be back in Pittsburgh and he'd return to Seattle, and that would be that.

Unless she quit the company.

That was a definite possibility, one she'd have to consider seriously. But not quite yet.

For now she needed to focus all her strength on getting through the upcoming weeks. Her feeling of dread was building with each day and while Annie had been reassuring, Rae still couldn't help but fear that something terrible was going to happen when she tried to give birth to this baby. After all, her own mother…

No. She wasn't going to think about that.

At the beach, Rae spread out her blanket and sat down. She was earlier than usual, and she had the entire cove to herself. She inhaled deeply, trying to convince herself how peaceful this all was, but instead she just felt lonely.

At thirty-two, she knew a few things about herself. She might not be the most lovable woman, but she was definitely smart. She'd traded on her intelligence all her life. She couldn't be stupid now. And to fall for Aidan, all over again, would be the dumbest thing she could do.

Still, his kindness the day before had felt genuine. He'd made her dinner. Fetched her favorite newspapers from town. Even made her herbal tea before bed, claiming it would help her sleep. Of course, all it had really accomplished was to make her need to go to the bathroom twice in the middle of the night.

And then there'd been those moments when he'd been looking at her, and she was sure she could see in his eyes some of the emotion—the caring and the affection—that she'd thought she'd seen that night in Philadelphia.

Rae sank down on the blanket and closed her eyes. The sun on her shoulders felt so soothing…like a mother's hands. Not that her mother's hands had ever been soothing.

She remembered a time when she'd been about the same age as that little boy they'd met on the beach. She'd been really sick, with a high fever and vomiting. Her mother had wanted her to go to school anyway, and she'd forced Rae out the door.

At school, Rae's teacher had put her hands on Rae's forehead. Her touch had been soft and gentle. "You're burning up, dear. You need to lie down."

At that moment Rae had wished more than anything that that teacher could be her real mother. Maybe there'd been a mix-up at the hospital or maybe she'd been adopted.

Sadly, she hadn't been adopted, and she'd been stuck with her own mother for many years to come.

But that wasn't going to happen to *her* baby. Her baby would have a mother who would feel her forehead if she had a fever and keep her home from school and not be annoyed about it.

Rae dozed for a short while, until the sound of children playing nearby woke her. She propped herself on her elbows and scanned the beach.

No sign of Nessa or Autumn today. Nor Tyler.

She felt sad thinking of the little boy. She was pretty sure that his father wasn't the type to feel his forehead for a fever, either.

With a sigh, she gathered the blanket and prepared to head home. After checking her watch, she picked up her pace. She hadn't realized she'd slept so long. She'd need to hurry to make her doctor's appointment at one.

By the time she reached the summerhouse, she was a little dizzy from the heat and exertion. Aidan held the door open for her.

"Our appointment's in half an hour," he said, his voice tight with disapproval.

Our appointment? He'd taken ownership of this pregnancy mighty quickly. *Guilt,* she reminded herself. That was why he was overdoing it now.

"It's only a ten-minute drive," she replied, slipping past him for the stairs. She headed for the bathroom, showered quickly, and then slid a dress over her head. Did Aidan think he could make up for eight months of absence by becoming her shadow now?

What good did he think he was going to do, anyway? She'd made it this far on her own. Of course, she still had the biggest hurdle of her pregnancy before her.

Labor.

She tried to clamp down on the feeling of terror, before it started to build. If her mother's stories were to be believed…

"Rae? Are you ready?"

"Hang on." Why was he rushing her? She had…she checked the time…oh, no, she had no time at all. Slipping her feet into her sandals, she dashed to the hall.

Aidan offered to drive and Rae decided to

let him. That way, if there were no parking spaces free, he could let her out in front of the medical clinic. Maybe by the time he'd parked, she'd already be in an examining room.

But there were several spaces right next to the clinic, and she and Aidan ended up entering the cozy reception area together.

The clinic was not a place where Rae felt comfortable. The walls were covered with reproduction paintings of kids and families, mothers and babies, puppies and kittens. A playroom, replete with nylon play castle and tunnel, dominated one corner of the room. The coffee table was covered with old issues of magazines that held absolutely no interest for her.

Today, with Aidan accompanying her, Rae felt even more self-conscious than she had on her previous visit. She could see the veiled curiosity in the receptionist's expression as the uniformed woman glanced from Aidan to Rae, then back again.

"Hello, Rae. I have an examining room ready for you. Would your partner like to come with you?"

"Yes, Irene," Aidan said smoothly. "That would be great."

Irene? Did he know her? Or had he just read the name on the silver pin the woman wore on her collar? A pin that Rae had just noticed this minute.

She felt Aidan touch her elbow. "That is, if it's okay with you?"

"Oh fine."

Irene's eyebrows flew up, and Rae guessed she'd sounded less than gracious. She didn't care. She wasn't out to win any popularity contests on this island—or anywhere else.

As on her previous visit, Rae's weight was taken before Irene led the two of them to one of the small examining rooms. Rae perched on the table and tried to pretend she didn't have a stomach the size of a watermelon.

"Dr. Marshall must be new to the island," Aidan said. He, like Rae, seemed to be doing his best to ignore the part of her anatomy the doctor was about to examine. "I spent my fair share of time in this clinic when I was a boy, but I don't remember her."

The doctor seemed as safe a subject as any. "Justine told me that Dr. Marshall moved here about five years ago. She used to work in emergency at Vancouver General."

There was a tap on the door, then it swung open. Dr. Marshall gave Rae a warm smile, and managed to look only mildly surprised at finding a man in the room, as well.

Rae introduced them without going into specifics. But when Dr. Marshall held out her hand to Aidan, she asked pointedly, "Are you the baby's father?"

"Yes, I am."

"Good. I'm glad you're here. I think Rae will need some support when the big day comes."

Right. As if Aidan was going to be any help. He was as clueless as she was—if not more so.

Rae submitted to the doctor's examination, feeling, as always, mildly violated by the procedure. Nothing against the doctor's bedside procedure—she was both respectful and gentle—but Rae still felt as if her body had been hijacked on her.

She hadn't planned for this baby and she wasn't prepared to deal with it. She longed for the day when this would all be behind her. But before that happened, she had to somehow get the baby out of her uterus and into the real world.

"How big do you think the baby is now?"

"I'd only be guessing, but I'd say around six pounds."

Phew. Six pounds wasn't too bad. She didn't want it to be undersize or anything, but she definitely didn't want to have to push out a ten-pound wonder, either.

Dr. Marshall withdrew her hand as the baby delivered a forceful kick.

"Hey! I could see that!" Aidan sounded delighted.

"Want to listen to the heartbeat?" the doctor offered.

No. He doesn't. Rae pressed her lips together to keep from saying the words out loud and sounding like a class A bitch.

But of course, that was probably exactly what she was. She didn't want Aidan listening to the baby's heartbeat. Nor did she want to see his eyes round with wonder, as they were already doing now. Or have him reach out a hand to her bare belly…then draw it back without touching her, as if he could sense her hostility to everything that was happening.

Rae squeezed her eyes shut. The problem was that she had no control in this situation. None at all. The baby was inside her and there was absolutely nothing she could do, but wait until it was ready to come out.

She was a grown woman. Yet, she felt like a scared little child who wanted her mommy. Only Mommy was gone now, not just emotionally absent but truly dead and gone.

"Everything looks great, Rae. I'm glad you're taking such good care of yourself and your baby." Dr. Marshall held out a hand to help her from her prone position. "I think we should talk a little about what will happen when you go into labor."

Rae's heart lurched. "Do you think it's going to happen soon?"

"According to your dates, not for another three weeks. But it could be earlier, and it could be later."

"Medical science is so helpful."

Dr. Marshall showed no reaction. "You said you'd taken prenatal classes in Pittsburgh?"

Rae could feel Aidan's eyes on her as she nodded.

"Then you know what to be on the lookout for. Once your contractions are between ten and five minutes apart, or if your water breaks, you should head here at once. If it's after hours, call the emergency number. Irene will give you a card."

"Okay." Rae put her hands on her kneecaps, hoping that neither the doctor nor Aidan had noticed her trembling. "So, are we all done?"

"All done. Get as much rest as possible, Rae." The doctor glanced at Aidan. "And if you'd like to help her, I'm sure a few foot massages would help bring down her swelling."

"Foot massages," Aidan repeated. "Right. No problem."

As they left the clinic, it was Aidan who remembered to stop and ask Irene for a card listing the emergency number. Not until they were back in his car, did he suddenly seem overwhelmed by the experience. Dropping his head to the steering wheel, he said, "Hell. There really is a baby inside you, Rae."

"Thanks for the news flash." She leaned

back on the headrest and closed her eyes. Three more weeks, according to the doctor. Could she take three more weeks of being pregnant?

More importantly, could she handle three more weeks of being around Aidan without letting him see how she really felt?

THE MESSAGE LIGHT on the Kincaids' phone was flashing when Aidan walked into the kitchen. He'd offered to make Rae tea, but she'd refused. Instead, she'd gone straight from his car to her bedroom.

The doctor's appointment had upset her, although Aidan wasn't sure why. He hoped it wasn't his presence in the examining room. But he was glad he'd gone. He wished he'd been with her from the beginning, and he could tell the doctor had thought so, as well. Rae had gone through too much on her own, for too long.

He'd give her some time to settle down, then he'd bring dinner up to her room on a tray. He opened the fridge, and frowned at the contents.

Maybe he should order in.

First, however, he needed to check for messages. There could be a problem at work.

But it turned out the call had been from Dex Ulrich. The detachment chief wanted Rae or Aidan to phone him immediately.

Aidan punched in the number and was put straight through.

"Thanks for calling, Aidan," the RCMP officer said. "I need to interview everyone who saw Tyler Jenkins yesterday."

"The little blond kid on the beach?" Aidan sank to a nearby chair, suddenly filled with dread. "What's wrong? Has something happened to him?"

"He didn't show up at home last night. This morning his father reported him missing."

CHAPTER SEVEN

RAE BARELY MADE IT from Aidan's car to her room before she began to weep. She grabbed a handful of tissues from the box on the dresser and glared at her reflection.

What is the matter with you, Rae Cordell? You never cry. Never.

She flopped onto the bed and stared at the ceiling while sopping up her tears. The drive home from the clinic had seemed to take forever. Aidan kept wanting to talk about the baby, and she'd barely managed to grunt her replies.

Letting him come along had been a big mistake. She'd have to sneak out on her own next week, assuming he was still here. Maybe a business emergency would call him back to Seattle before then... At least she could always hope that's what would happen.

Rae rolled onto her side, and stuffed a pillow under her belly. She could do this. She only had three more weeks. Then it would be over and she could get back to work. Quitting Kincaid Communications seemed to be her only option now. She needed to make a fresh start.

Where would she like to live? Not Seattle. Maybe San Francisco? She could call a headhunter and...

Just like that, an image of Aidan's face when he'd been listening to the baby's heartbeat popped into her head. She'd never forget the wonder in his eyes. His delighted surprise when he'd actually seen the baby moving in her belly.

"Ohh..." She was crying again, damn it. But it wasn't about Aidan. It couldn't be. She was just worried about the labor. Her mother had hemorrhaged when Rae was born and she had almost died.

Rae's mother had told the story. Often. And always concluded with the warning: "Just wait until you have a baby. Then you'll know how much I suffered."

Rae didn't want to know. She didn't want

to have this baby. A baby she couldn't even keep because...

"Rae?" Aidan rapped on her bedroom door. "Can I talk to you a minute?"

She pushed her face into the pillow so he couldn't hear her crying and waited for him to leave.

"Rae?" He knocked again.

He didn't seem likely to go away until she responded. She cleared her throat, then called back at him, "I'm busy."

"It's important. I'll wait."

Oh, for crying out loud... And then, because she *had* been crying out loud, Rae started to laugh. She heaved her body off the bed and went over to the mirror. She blotted her eyes and blew her nose. She still looked like hell, but what could she do?

Taking a deep breath, she twisted the handle and pulled. "I was sleeping. Couldn't this have wait—"

"Rae." Aidan grabbed her free hand. "We had a message from Dex Ulrich at the RCMP detachment. The little boy we met on the beach yesterday, Tyler Jenkins?"

Rae caught her breath. Aidan looked

deadly serious and she was suddenly afraid. "Yes?"

Aidan let go of her hand gently. "Tyler didn't make it home last night. His father has reported him missing."

Missing.

Her first thought was of the ocean. She covered her mouth. "Surely he didn't..."

Aidan shook his head, guessing what she meant. "I don't think he'd have gone in the water. He didn't like getting wet, remember?"

"Yes." Relief, sweet relief, made her head feel lighter. "That's right. He didn't."

Other, less scary possibilities began to occur to her. Tyler might have spent the night with a friend. Or become lost and been unable to find his way home. That was a little more frightening, but not as bad as drowning in the ocean.

"The thing is, Rae, Dex wants to question us. I'm guessing we may have been among the last people to see Tyler before he disappeared."

"Really?"

He nodded. "I know you're tired, but do you think we could go there right now?"

"Of course." She'd tossed her purse on the bureau earlier, and now she retrieved it and followed Aidan down the stairs.

On the drive back to Cedarbrae, Rae tried to recall details that might be helpful. Aidan was silent, too, and she imagined that his thoughts, like hers, were focused on the missing boy.

Tyler was only six years old. He shouldn't have been wandering around the island unsupervised in the first place. But he had been. And now this was the result.

Could he have been abducted? Murdered? Rae tried to close her mind to these darkest of possibilities. Surely such horrific crimes didn't happen in idyllic places like Summer Island.

Aidan swung his car into a parking stall beside the RCMP detachment, then dashed around to help Rae lever her body out of the low-slung seat. She kept a hand to her lower back as she made the gravity-defying maneuver, brushing against Aidan briefly once she had both feet on pavement.

"You okay?" Aidan steadied her with a hand to her shoulder. "I'm sorry I had to wake you. You look tired."

She should have worn sunglasses to hide her red eyes. "I'm fine, Aidan. This is way more important."

Still, he kept an arm loosely around her waist as they walked round to the entrance of the building. The front desk officer seemed to be expecting them. He nodded and opened the door that led to the back offices.

"Sergeant Ulrich's waiting for you."

They headed past a bull pen, where a lone officer sat leaning over a telephone, speaking intently.

"Are you sure you didn't see him? A little boy, six years old, with blond hair and blue…"

The desk clerk opened the door to Dex's office and waved them inside. Ulrich was on the phone, as well. He nodded at the two available chairs and continued with his questioning, which was clearly related to the lost little boy.

He hung up with a decided air of dissatisfaction.

"You haven't found him?" Aidan was on the edge of his chair, his forehead lined with worry.

"Afraid not. The last reported sighting was on Pebble Beach yesterday around noon."

So Aidan had been right. They *were* the most recent witnesses.

"I've already spoken to Nessa Brooke. She said the last she saw Tyler was when he was sitting on your blanket eating an apple."

"That's right. I asked him what his phone number was, so I could call his father. He said he wanted to keep playing and ran off," Aidan said.

"Did you notice what Tyler did next?" Ulrich looked at them expectantly.

"Sorry, Dex. I lost sight of him," Aidan said. "I've been racking my brain, but I can't remember anything."

Hope faded in the sergeant's eyes. "Rae? Did you see anything else?"

"No. I wish I could help, but I didn't see anything else, either."

"You didn't notice anyone approaching Tyler?"

"No," they said in concert.

"Did you see anyone on the beach, anyone at all, who seemed to stand out or didn't seem to belong?"

At the officer's prodding, Rae and Aidan described everyone they could remember who had been on the beach that day. There were no men, other than Dex Ulrich himself, on the list. Without exception, the others had all been mothers and children.

"What about Tyler's clothes? Can you recall what he was wearing? I just want to confirm my own recollection."

"A red T-shirt," Rae said quickly.

Aidan nodded. "And cutoff blue jeans. Bare feet."

Rae thought of another detail that hadn't been mentioned. Would it matter? She had no idea, but she couldn't leave this room without saying anything.

"Sergeant Ulrich, both Aidan and I noticed that Tyler had bruises on his wrists."

"That's right," Aidan said. "Must have been a real firm grip, to leave those kinds of marks."

Ulrich had been pretty restrained until that moment, but now Rae saw a flash of emotion. Anger, quickly concealed.

"I'm not surprised." A note of weariness crept into his voice. "We've had a number of complaints about that boy's father over the past year."

"Why hasn't anyone done anything about it, then?" Rae wanted to know.

"Each time a complaint was made, a social worker visited the home. But removing a child from his biological parent is always the last resort, Rae. I guess the caseworker thought the situation was under control."

"What happened to his mother?" Aidan asked. "Tyler told us she was dead."

"That's right. Amanda Jenkins died of cancer a year ago. Ted was always a little rough around the edges, but after he lost his wife he really started drinking. As you can imagine, a full-blown substance-abuse problem hasn't helped the home situation."

"Poor Tyler," Aidan said.

"Yeah. It's been tough on the kid." Ulrich made a series of quick checkmarks in his open notebook, then clicked the top of his pen and set it down.

"That's it for now," he told them. "If I have any more questions I'll call you at the Kincaid place. You'll be around for a few more weeks?"

Rae wondered if she imagined the sergeant's gaze dropping briefly to her belly. In her situation—unmarried, unattached—her pregnancy frequently seemed to be the unmentioned elephant in the room.

Today, however, Tyler's disappearance made her personal problems pale in comparison.

"I'll be on the island until the baby's born."

"So will I."

She glanced at Aidan, and found him already watching her. There was something in his expression she'd never seen before. Something possessive. And protective. It made her feel breathless, light-headed.

Afraid.

She turned back to Dex Ulrich. He'd been flipping pages in his notebook, unaware of the little moment she'd just shared with the father of her baby.

Tyler. Her thoughts jerked back to the missing boy. So little to be on his own for an entire night. Could he just be missing—perhaps lost in one of the island's dense forested areas?

"Is there anything we can do to help?" Aidan asked.

"Just keep an eye out. We've got our Emergency Response team working already and another unit's expected from Saltspring later this afternoon."

"What about search parties?" Aidan asked.

Dex nodded. "My team is organizing local volunteers as we speak. We've got a temporary command post set up on Pebble Beach, since that's where the boy was last seen."

Dex placed his hands on the surface of his desk, then pushed himself into a standing position. "Thanks again for coming in. I'll see you out."

The officer in the bull pen was still on the phone as Rae and Aidan left the office. He nodded to his commanding officer, eyed Rae with mild curiosity, and then continued making notes.

Ulrich opened a locked door that separated the public space from the rest of the detachment. "Call, if you think of anything else that might be helpful."

"We will," Rae said. "I hope you find Tyler soon."

The entrance door swung open then, and Nessa Brooke rushed inside. She was flushed, and from the outfit she was wearing Rae guessed she'd come straight from a workout. Perhaps at the yoga studio in the house across the street from the Kincaid summerhouse.

"Dex! Is there any news?" Nessa was breathless, distraught.

The officer offered her a comforting arm. "I'm afraid not."

"Doesn't anyone have any idea what happened to him?"

"Not so far. Tyler just seems to have…vanished."

"Oh, God." She covered her eyes for a moment. "I should have kept a closer eye on him on the beach yesterday. Driven him home, so I'd have known he got there safely."

"Don't, Nessa. Please don't blame yourself. Even if you had given him a ride, his father would have let him walk out the door alone five minutes later."

"Yes, but…" Suddenly Nessa seemed to notice that she and the sergeant weren't alone. "Aidan. Rae. Isn't this terrible?"

"Yes." Rae nodded. Terrible pretty much summed it up.

"You hear about children going missing in big cities. But Summer Island!" Nessa turned back to Ulrich. "What can I do, Dex? I need to help find him."

"The most likely scenario is that Tyler is lost somewhere between the beach and his home. We've got search parties combing that area now."

"I can help…."

"No, Nessa." Dex glanced briefly at her legs, and Rae guessed that Nessa's multiple sclerosis was on his mind. "We already have lots of volunteers for that job. Why don't you pay a visit to Tyler's father? See how Ted's holding up?"

"Would you like some company?" Rae offered. She was too pregnant to be of much help with the search party, either. But like Nessa, she didn't relish the idea of sitting at home and doing nothing.

"Yes, I would." Nessa sounded genuinely grateful for the offer.

"I'll join the volunteers on the beach," Aidan said. "I know the south end of the island very well. We used to play there all the time as kids."

"That would be great." Dex turned to Nessa and lowered his voice. "I don't want you to overdo things, okay? After you talk to Ted, go home and rest. I'll drop by your place with an update as soon as I can."

"For heaven's sake, don't worry about me, Dex. Rae and I will be fine, won't we?" The petite woman linked her arm with Rae's and started forward. "My car is parked outside. Okay if we take that?"

AIDAN'S GIRLFRIEND—if that's what she was—remained quiet for most of the drive to the Jenkins's house. She was a beauty, this Rae Cordell, and smart as a whip according to Harrison. He and Justine believed Aidan and Rae would make a perfect match.

But from the two times Nessa had seen them together, she was guessing the expecting couple hadn't realized it yet.

"So, when's your baby due?"

It had seemed like a safe question to ask, but Rae practically scowled. "Three weeks."

"I'll bet you'll be glad to have that over

with. Being pregnant in the summer heat must be tough."

Rae snorted softly. "The heat's the least of it."

"Huh?" Nessa slowed as she approached a four-way stop. Ted and Tyler Jenkins lived to the left, well in from the coveted waterfront properties on the east side of the island. Farther north, the terrain became much more rugged, almost impassable.

"I just mean that everything about being pregnant is hard."

"Really?" Nessa tried not to be judgmental, but it was difficult for her. The years she'd spent longing to conceive! "I was married for six years. We wanted children, but it didn't happen."

Rae looked startled by the revelation. "I'm sorry to hear that."

"It's okay." But it was painful to remember how miserable she'd felt every month when her hopes were dashed. She'd always loved children. Plus, she'd secretly hoped that a baby would save her marriage to Gabe. "Since our marriage didn't last, it probably worked out for the best. At least, that's what

I tell myself. But I have to admit, whenever I see a pregnant woman, I still feel a little envious."

Rae gave her an incredulous look but said nothing.

Nessa spotted a dilapidated bungalow to the left. The mailbox out front looked like someone had given it a vicious kick, almost, but not quite, uprooting it from the ground. In faded letters, the name Jenkins could just be made out on the dented metal surface.

"I guess we're here." A rusted truck was parked in the drive and Nessa stopped her car behind it. She started to open the door, but a word from Rae stopped her.

"Nessa? I want you to know something."

Rae paused and Nessa was surprised to see her face grow a little pink. Rae seemed too self-controlled to suffer from ordinary embarrassment. And yet, that's exactly what she seemed to be experiencing right now.

"I'm giving up the baby when it's born," she finally blurted out.

Nessa didn't know what to say. Her first instinct was to ask, why? But she guessed that wouldn't be construed as supportive.

"I just wanted that clear," Rae said. Abruptly, she turned and got out of the car.

It was clear all right. Clear as mud. What was with this person? Some women didn't know how lucky they were.

Rae reached the front door before Nessa did. She knocked loudly, but there was no answer. Rae knocked a second time, and after another long pause, Nessa was about to suggest they leave, when Rae grasped the doorknob.

"It isn't locked."

"Yes, but…"

"The truck is here. He must be home." Rae opened the door. Entered the house.

The lack of an invitation was not holding her back. "Rae, are you sure…"

"There's no one in the living room."

Nessa heard footsteps disappearing down the hall. What was Rae doing? She had no right to enter someone else's house uninvited.

Was Rae worried that Ted had hurt himself? Nessa decided to follow her, passing through the dark hallway into a grimy-looking kitchen. Rae stopped by the fridge, planted her hands on her hips and looked disgusted.

"What's—" As Nessa moved forward, she saw the man slumped at the kitchen table and gasped. "Is he dead?"

"God, no." Rae wrinkled her nose. "He's passed out, that's all. Can't you smell the alcohol?"

CHAPTER EIGHT

"HE LOOKS DEAD TO ME." Nessa, still at the kitchen entrance, pressed a hand to her mouth.

Disgusted at the sight of Tyler's drunken father, Rae picked up a glass from the counter, rinsed it clean and filled it with cold water. She crossed the room and tossed the contents on his head.

Nessa was the first to react. "Rae!"

Finally, Ted Jenkins stirred. "Huh?" Slowly, he lifted his head from the table, then used his hands to prop himself up.

"See?" Rae said. "Not dead."

"Oh, my. You were right." Nessa stared at Ted Jenkins for a moment, and then started to shake.

The trembling worried Rae. Was this a side effect of MS? She'd read somewhere that stress could aggravate symptoms of the disease. And then she looked at Nessa's face more closely and realized she was just plain angry.

"How could you do this?" Nessa advanced on Ted, her hands clenched in fists. "Your son is *missing*. Half the people on this island are out looking for him. And you're sitting at home drinking!"

She turned from Ted to Rae, shaking her head. "Can you believe this?"

"His behavior does not suggest much parental concern." Rae realized that beneath the mild and sweet demeanor, Nessa was tougher than she'd first seemed. Clearly, Rae had underestimated the woman. Bad judgment on her part, since this was Harrison's sister, and next to Aidan, Harrison was the most determined, tenacious man Rae had ever met.

"Huh?" Ted said again. He shook the water out of his hair, then groaned and clutched his head.

"What if Tyler had walked in that door right now, instead of us?" Nessa planted her fists on her hips. "What if he's been trying to phone you for help?"

"Tyler." Something was finally getting through the man's alcoholic haze. "My boy. He's missing."

"Brilliant deduction, Watson." Rae went to stand by Nessa, mostly because she was afraid the other woman might punch Ted Jenkins. Given that Nessa weighed a hundred pounds at the most, and Ted obviously used his brawn to earn a living, Rae thought that was an encounter best avoided.

Ted rubbed his eyes, then focused on the pair of them. He pointed at Nessa. "You, I recognize. Who's she?"

He stared at Rae. Briefly at her face, and then longer at her belly.

"I'm Rae Cordell, vice president of operations at Kincaid Communication's Pittsburgh division."

He stared, befuddled, and then slammed his hand on the table. "Well, whoever you are, you don't have no business in my house. You neither, Nessa."

"Excuse me, Mr. Jenkins. We were just trying to be helpful. We wanted to offer you moral support." Rae picked up the empty bottle of rye and turned it upside down. "But I see you've found your comfort elsewhere."

"Give that to me." He grabbed the bottle from her hands. "Easy for you to judge. You don't know the hell I've been going through."

Ted Jenkins stood up, using a hand on the table to keep his body steady. He was almost six feet tall; the thin, wiry sort of man who was generally stronger than he looked. He hadn't shaved in several days and his hair was so dirty it was difficult to identify the color, but Rae thought it was probably a medium brown when it was clean.

"Are you sure Tyler isn't hiding at home somewhere?" Nessa's tone had turned gently conciliatory. "Little kids will do that sometimes, won't they?"

Ted's shoulders slumped a little, as a bit of the fight left him. "I've already looked, and so did Dex early this morning. Didn't find any sign of the boy."

"I suppose you've already made a list of Tyler's friends? Places he might have gone to play?"

Ted waved his hands, as if shooing off flies. "Yeah, yeah, I gone through all that with Dex." He arched his back, which was probably aching after sleeping at the table in that way. Then he ambled to the kitchen sink, adjusted the temperature of the taps, and splashed water over his face. After drying himself on a nearby towel, he turned to glower at them once more.

"You planning on watching me shave, too?"

In the kitchen? He was going to shave in the kitchen? Rae scanned the countertop and saw a razor and a can of shaving gel next to the dish soap.

She turned to Nessa, who was staring at Jenkins as if he was a rare creature from the wild.

Rae put a hand on Nessa's shoulder. She didn't think Ted could shower in here, too, but she didn't want to take that chance. "I'd say our work here is done. Let's get out of Mr. Jenkins's hair, shall we?"

Nessa nodded and began to retreat. Then she paused and said, "You'll call me if you need anything?"

Jenkins, his face covered in white foam, just grunted.

Rae was pretty sure he wouldn't call.

"YOU WERE COOL as a cucumber in there." With new respect, Nessa addressed the high-powered MBA her brother had raved about.

"Yeah?"

Rae was sitting in the passenger seat of Nessa's car with her head twisted slightly so that Nessa couldn't see her face clearly. But there was a weight to Rae's one-word response that made Nessa suspect the encounter had been harder on Rae than she'd let on.

"I wouldn't have had the courage to walk through that front door, let alone toss water in his face." And Rae had done it so calmly, as if rousing drunks was something…

Oh. Nessa let her eyes leave the road for a second as she stole another gaze at her companion. Rae's hands were clenched atop her knees, knuckles white.

Okay, so there was definitely more to this woman than she'd realized. She'd cut Rae some slack about her decision to give up her baby. Maybe Rae had a good reason.

Nessa couldn't imagine what it might be, but she was willing to give Rae the benefit of the doubt.

"Do you think Ted even cares that his son is missing?" she asked Rae.

"It doesn't look like it. But maybe we shouldn't judge him too harshly. He's under a lot of stress, and that's always a trigger for someone with a drinking problem."

"I suppose."

"On the other hand, Aidan and I saw bruises on Tyler's wrists yesterday."

"Oh, no." Nessa wondered why she hadn't picked up on that. Probably, because she'd been paying too much attention to Dex. She felt her cheeks grow hot, and now she pressed one palm to the side of her face.

"You know these people better than I do, Nessa. Do you think Ted is physically abusive to Tyler?"

"I've had concerns in the past. But mostly about Tyler's diet and hygiene. His dad would drop him off at day care and it would be obvious he hadn't given his son a bath or fed him breakfast. Over this past year I called social services several times, and I know a caseworker has been working with Ted to help him cope since Amanda's death."

Nessa slowed the car as she approached

the Kincaid summerhouse. She pulled in behind Rae's rental and stopped the engine.

Was it possible Tyler had been more than neglected?

"Did you tell Dex about the bruises?"

"Yes."

"I wonder if Tyler might have run away from home because he was afraid of his father?"

"Yes. Or—" Rae stopped, obviously unwilling to put into words the possibility that Ted could have seriously harmed his young son.

"Surely Ted couldn't be such a monster."

"I hope not." Rae slipped out of the car. "Thanks for dropping me home. Let me know if you hear anything."

"I will, Rae." Nessa waved goodbye, then got out her phone and dialed Dex's cell. In the past, her ex-husband hadn't been available to take her calls. Not that she was comparing Dex to Gabe. It was just...nice to have a friend she could count on.

Dex answered on the first ring, and she sighed with relief. "Rae and I just got back from Ted Jenkins's place. I thought I'd fill you in."

"I'd like that Ness, but I'm headed back to Pebble Beach right now. Can you meet me there?"

RAE WENT IN through the front door. The house was silent; the air felt cool. She wondered if there'd been any news about Tyler, but there were no messages on the machine. It had been good of Aidan to volunteer to join the search party when he hardly knew the boy.

Aidan was as concerned about the little guy as she was. Strange, really, given that they'd only met Tyler the once.

But the Summer Island residents were a small, tightly knit group, and it seemed right for them to rally together with the other citizens and do whatever they could to help. Especially since it seemed they were the last people to have seen Tyler before he disappeared.

Rae wandered the main floor restlessly. She hated feeling useless, yet she knew it would be ridiculous for her to join the search party. At this stage in her pregnancy, she'd be more of a liability than a help. But she couldn't just sit here and wait for news. She'd go crazy.

She needed something to keep her busy.

Maybe she should pay a visit to Jennifer's Aunt Annie. The older woman had sounded willing to continue their conversation. Rae didn't really want to talk about babies, but there was something about Annie that she liked. Most people got all sentimental when they talked about motherhood and babies.

Annie wasn't like that. She was practical and no-nonsense. Maybe she'd have some useful advice on coping with labor. Rae opened the local phone directory and called Lavender Farm. Annie invited her to come right over.

THE PARKING LOT at Pebble Beach was full, so Nessa had to leave her car on the side of the road and walk down to the beach. For the first time in a long while her left leg was feeling stiff. She favored it slightly as she made her way toward a group of people that included Dex and another RCMP officer she didn't recognize, all of them standing next to Dex's cruiser.

Just seeing Dex, a figure of authority in his uniform and aviator sunglasses, gave her a measure of comfort. Solid, dependable Dex would do everything possible to find Tyler.

She was close enough to call out to him, when he spotted her. For a moment, a smile erased the creases of worry around his mouth. But the smile evaporated all too quickly. After giving instructions to the officer next to him, he left the others and came to her.

He lifted the sunglasses for a moment to study her. "Nessa, you shouldn't be here. You look exhausted."

She glanced at the people around them. "Everyone's tired, Dex. Even you." She touched his arm, suddenly concerned that he was pushing himself too hard. "Have you had anything to eat since this started?"

"I'm fine. Don't worry about me."

He didn't say anything further, but she heard the underlying message. Dex didn't have MS. She did. Therefore, she couldn't be expected to carry the same load as other people.

Generally, Nessa had come to terms with

the diagnosis of a year ago. But when people tried to impose unnecessary restrictions on her activities, she resented the hell out of her illness.

"I wanted to tell you about Ted Jenkins. Rae and I went to see him as you suggested."

Dex looked interested. "And?"

"He was drunk. Out cold."

"Ah, hell. I should have guessed he might hit the bottle. I'm sorry I sent you out there, Nessa."

"Do you think he even *cares* that his son is missing?"

"I imagine he does. He sounded worried when he called me early this morning."

"But to get so drunk…"

"Drinking is how men like Ted Jenkins handle stress."

"Okay. But what about the bruises? Did Aidan and Rae tell you about those?"

His lips tightened and he nodded. "When this is over, Ted'll have to account for any mark we find on that boy's body."

When this is over. But how would it end? Nessa couldn't stand to think of any outcome other than a favorable one. "Rae and I were wondering if Tyler might have run away from home."

"Because he was afraid of his father?"

She nodded.

"That's one possibility. It might even be the most likely scenario. However, we've already spoken to the families of all his school chums and playmates. No one saw him yesterday, at all."

"So now what?"

"Mostly, it'll be footwork at this stage. You go on home and get some rest. We've got plenty of volunteers."

"But—" Movement from the far end of the beach caught her eye. "Looks like one of the search groups is back."

About fifteen men and women, including a few older teenagers, as well, rounded the corner of the boardwalk. Their trudging pace indicated they had no good news to report.

Leading the pack was Aidan Wythe. He looked tired and discouraged—his jeans were dirty and his face wasn't all that clean, either. Still, he managed to look gorgeous, as usual.

As a teen, Nessa had idolized all her brother's friends, but it was the blond, outgoing

Gabe she'd set her heart on. After years of trying to catch his attention, she'd finally succeeded the summer Harrison and Simone were married. Her wedding to Gabe had followed soon after, but their life together had never lived up to her fantasy.

Watching Aidan now, she wondered what would have happened if she'd fallen for him, instead of Gabe. In many ways, Aidan was Gabe's opposite: dark-haired, quiet, almost broody. People often complained that he was a difficult man to get to know.

It took a lot for him to warm up to someone new.

But once Aidan committed himself—whether to a friend, like Harrison, or a cause, like trying to find a lost boy—he was one hundred percent committed. Many times, Harrison had told her that he would trust Aidan with anything. And she knew he could, too.

When Aidan found the right woman, he was going to be a loyal, devoted husband. So far, it hadn't happened. Could Rae be the one?

"I'd better get back to work," Dex said. "I'll call you later?"

She nodded, then watched him walk

forward to meet the incoming group. He stopped in front of Aidan, and they spoke briefly. After a few minutes, the discussion seemed to take a slightly argumentative turn.

She could guess what was going on. While the rest of the group was slowly dispersing, Aidan was insisting that he would go out and look for Tyler again. Undoubtedly, Dex was telling him to go home and get some food and rest.

Wasn't that just like Aidan, to give so much in a search for a boy he barely knew?

The two men finally stopped talking. Dex jogged back to the police cruiser, while a dejected Aidan headed her way.

She met him halfway. "Let me guess. Dex told you to go home, and you're not happy about it."

One side of Aidan's mouth lifted slightly. "You know me too well."

"For the record, Dex is right this time. You've already done so much. Some vacation, huh?"

Aidan used the hem of his T-shirt to wipe the grime from his face. "That was already a lost cause."

So he wasn't impressed with Harrison and Justine's matchmaking efforts. "You could always leave and go somewhere else for the rest of your holiday."

"No, I can't."

"Because of the baby?"

He nodded.

So it *was* his, then. Harrison and Justine had been right. "Rae says she plans to give it up."

Aidan took a moment to consider his response. "She's pretty serious about her career."

Nessa imagined that Rae's thought processes were a little more complicated than that, but she didn't dispute his statement. "How do you feel about that? About the baby going up for adoption."

He shrugged. "I'm not sure how to feel. I only found out Rae was pregnant two days ago."

Two days ago? "How is that possible?"

He looked a little sheepish. "We haven't had a very typical relationship."

No kidding.

Aidan gave her a playful nudge. "So what's up with you and Dex?"

The question startled her. Embarrassed her. "We're just friends...."

He laughed. "Yeah, right. I've seen the way you two look at each other."

"You're imagining things."

"And you're *blushing*."

She punched him lightly on the arm. "Stop it. I'm serious, Aidan. Dex and I are friends, and that's it. Anything else wouldn't be fair to him."

Aidan's grin faded. "What are you talking about?"

"Don't play dumb. You know about my MS." She backed off a few paces. How had they started talking about this? She really didn't want to have this conversation. "Look, I've got to get—"

"Nessa..."

"See you later, Aidan." She turned and ran, praying her leg wouldn't give out on her right now.

CHAPTER NINE

AIDAN DROVE BACK to the summerhouse, scowling when he noticed Rae's car missing from its usual parking space. Where had she gone?

He was desperate for a shower and a cold beer, but what if she'd gone into early labor? He called the clinic and was relieved to hear that no one there had heard from her. As he hung up, he noticed that the phone book was open and the number for Lavender Farm had been circled.

Okay. At least she was safe.

He glanced around the deserted kitchen. The place didn't feel right without Rae there. He wandered out to the living room, pausing by the river rock fireplace. Once, there'd been several pictures of Simone on the mantel, but they'd been moved to make room for the framed photographs of Harrison and Justine's wedding.

They made an attractive couple. Justine's smile was full of confidence and sass, just like the woman herself. As for Harrison, he had the look of a man who had finally found peace and contentment...and was damn glad about it.

Aidan's gaze moved to the next photograph. Autumn had made a pretty flower girl. He glanced away from that picture quickly. The one beside it was of Aidan and Nessa. Nessa had been the matron of honor and he'd been Harrison's best man—for the second time. Hopefully this marriage would last longer and be happier than Harrison's first.

Aidan crossed the room, at first avoiding the concert-size grand piano, then finally going over to run his fingers up and down the scale of C major. It was the only thing he could play. If you counted scales as playing the piano.

This piano had once been Simone's, but he supposed it was Autumn's now. They said she was even more talented than her mother, but that was hard to imagine.

On the beach the other day she'd told him about some new songs she'd learned. He should have been more interested. Not brushed her off. Yet, he never managed to do or say the right thing around Autumn.

Aidan circled back to the kitchen, restless and bored. This was how things were supposed to have been on his so-called vacation. Maybe he should enjoy the illusion of peace while he had it.

He twisted the cap off a bottle of beer, snagged a bag of chips from the cupboard, and went out to the deck where he picked the most comfortable chair of the bunch.

The first swallow went down long and cool. Perfect. He leaned his head against the cushioned rest and contemplated another blue Summer Island sky.

This was the life. This was just great.

All he had to do was pretend a little boy wasn't missing and the coworker he'd had a one-night stand with eight months ago wasn't pregnant, and he'd be totally relaxed right now.

He took another swig of beer, grabbed a handful of corn chips and told himself he had nothing to worry about. The entire community was on the lookout for Tyler. The little boy was going to be okay. As for Rae—she seemed to have everything mapped out. All he needed to do was hang around for a few weeks until the situation was resolved.

Then they could go their separate ways and it would be as if none of this ever happened.

Aidan had another drink.

Yeah, right.

Truth was, Tyler's life was in jeopardy, and Aidan and Rae weren't even close to being okay, either.

He swung his legs off the chair and stood up. He was just kidding himself if he thought he could kick back and relax in the midst of all this. He paced to one end of the deck. Then the other. At the sound of a car on the road, he paused and listened carefully, but the car didn't stop, didn't even slow down.

How long was Rae planning to stay at Lavender Farm? Maybe he should swing by there. Just to make sure she really was okay.

THIRTY MINUTES LATER, after a rushed shower and a quick drive, Aidan parked his convertible next to Rae's rented sedan in the yard at Jennifer's bed-and-breakfast.

The scent of lavender and the contented humming of hundreds of bumblebees rose up in greeting as he skirted past the flower beds toward the front door. No one answered when he knocked, so he followed the path to the backyard.

He found Jennifer's aunt and Rae sitting on a cedar bench amidst a profusion of blossoms. Their backs were to Aidan, and they were talking earnestly. As he moved closer, Annie passed a jar to the pregnant woman.

"Lanolin," she said. "Rub this over your belly and your nipples every night."

He stopped short, assailed by a sudden, erotic image of Rae massaging cream into the skin of her swollen breasts and belly. Was he sick for finding the idea very arousing?

"What about labor?" Rae asked. "Do you have any magic potions to help with that?"

Annie laughed. "I'd be a millionaire if I did. But you're going to be fine." She patted Rae's shoulder. "I know you're scared. Trust me— every woman is frightened the first time."

Rae didn't answer at first. Then she said quietly, "My mother hemorrhaged when I was born. She nearly died."

What? Aidan had never considered that something might go wrong in the delivery. He held his breath, waiting to see what the midwife would say.

"That happens sometimes," Annie said in a matter-of-fact manner. "But just because your mother had problems doesn't mean you will, too. And remember—your mother didn't die. Is that what you're really afraid of Rae, dying?"

"Consciously, no. But on another level—maybe. This whole experience is so foreign to me. I never planned on having kids. I certainly never imagined I'd get pregnant."

"Fear is normal, even for women who are desperate to have a child. And it doesn't stop with delivery. Looking after babies can be a challenge, at first. You wouldn't believe the mothers I've coached through breast-feeding, for instance."

"Is it hard to do—breast-feeding?"

"Depends. Some babies figure it out right away. Others need a little help. The point is, women aren't born with instruction manuals for having children. That's why we need other women, experienced women, for guidance."

"Like you. Annie. You know so much."

"After all these years, I ought to." Annie held out her hands in front of her. Even from a distance, Aidan could see that the knuckles were swollen, the fingers twisted. "If it wasn't for this blasted arthritis, I'd still be working." She raised her voice. "You looking for someone, Aidan?"

Busted. Had the old midwife sensed his presence right from the beginning?

Rae twisted round to look at him. She didn't look pleased. "What are you doing here?"

"Looking for you." But now that he'd admitted that, he realized he'd backed himself into a corner. Why had it seemed so important to find Rae? She was an independent, grown woman. What she did with her time was no business of his. "Just wanted to make sure you hadn't gone into labor early or anything."

Rae grimaced. "Don't even *say* that."

She really was scared. The realization made him feel tender toward her. Something she undoubtedly wouldn't appreciate, if he was foolish enough to let her know.

He turned to Annie. "Where's Jennifer?"

"She and her father took the truck and went for a drive. Looking for that missing boy." Annie shook her head. Clearly, she didn't think that had been a good idea.

"Pretty much everyone on the island is joining in the hunt," he said.

"Has there been any news?" Rae asked.

"Not since I last spoke to Dex about two hours ago."

Rae sighed. "I suppose I should be heading back. Nessa said she'd call if there were any developments." As she began to lift her heavy body from the bench, Aidan sprang forward to offer a hand. He was surprised when she accepted it.

"That tea I promised you is in my cottage." Annie pointed to a cute building covered in cedar shingles, with pansies growing in the windowboxes. "I'll go get it and meet you at your car."

"We'll come with you," Rae said. "I'd love to see the inside of your cottage. It looks adorable from the outside."

Annie waved her off. "Another time. The place is a mess right now. Besides, your back is aching. You shouldn't be on your feet at all." She squinted at Aidan. "A foot rub tonight would be a good idea."

She was the second professional to make that suggestion. Aidan glanced at Rae to see if she looked receptive. "Would that be before or after the breast and belly massage?" he asked.

Rae jerked away from him. "How long were you standing there listening?"

"Long enough," Annie said. "Now don't you two drive off before I get you that tea...."

"OKAY, RAE. Doctor's orders and Annie's, too. It's time for your massage."

Aidan was sitting on the sofa, a cushion in his lap. Rae, fresh from the shower and dressed in a long cotton robe that was light enough for the warm evening, yet still gave her overripe body adequate coverage, looked at him warily. He had an open bottle of lavender moisturizer in his hands. At the last minute, Annie had given her that, as well as the tea that was supposed to help with indigestion.

"Did you check the messages?" she asked, stalling.

"Nessa called. There's no news."

"Damn." Rae glanced at the sky. The sun would be setting shortly. This would make the second night Tyler had been missing from his home.

"They'll find him, Rae," Aidan said gently. "I'm sure they'll find him."

"I hope you're right." Tentatively, she sat on the other end of the sofa. Aidan patted the cushion on his lap expectantly, and Rae drew up her legs.

Ordinarily, she'd have leaped at the chance to have her feet rubbed. But with Aidan she had to be cautious. She'd noticed that the closer she came to her due date, the more emotional she became. And emotions were something she needed to guard carefully where Aidan was concerned.

Still, she couldn't stop the tingle of pleasure that raced up her legs, when he placed her feet in his lap.

He squirted a dollop of cream into his hands, warmed it, then ran his palms from her right ankle to the tips of her toes.

Oh, God. Already this felt so good. Rae let her back relax against the cushions.

Aidan rubbed his thumb in a circular

pattern against her instep. Again, the shock waves traveled beyond her foot, up her leg, her spine, her neck....

"Cold?"

"A little." She wasn't, but she had to explain that shiver somehow.

He unfolded a soft throw and laid it over her belly. Then he encased her foot with both his hands and stroked the length of it. After doing this for several minutes, he began to work on each toe.

And the pleasurable impulses became decidedly erotic. She remembered the night they'd made love, how Aidan had trailed kisses from her throat to her belly.

It had been flat then, her belly. And he'd been moaning about her beautiful body as he'd helped himself to everything he wanted from it—which had been everything she'd wanted, too.

She groaned but didn't open her eyes.

"Other foot."

"Already? I was just getting into this," she lied. She'd been into it from the start. And she'd rather swallow her tongue than admit just *how* into it she'd been.

He shifted her right foot and made room for the left. "You're insatiable," he said. "How could I have forgotten?"

Her eyes flew open. "This is hardly the same thing."

"True."

Was it her imagination, or were his hands sliding a little farther up her calf this time? If so, Rae wasn't about to complain. She closed her eyes again and settled back onto the cushion.

"Rae, why didn't you tell me you were pregnant? When you first found out, I mean."

Her eyes sprang open. "You really know how to ruin a good massage."

"It must have been a shock," he persisted. "Didn't you want to talk to someone about it?"

"Maybe I did."

His hands stilled. "You mean you told someone else?"

She couldn't believe he had the nerve to look affronted. "You banished me to Pittsburgh. You didn't call, and you didn't write."

"For the last time, it was a *promotion*. And who did you tell?"

Who did he think she'd confided in? She knew no one in Pittsburgh and she certainly wasn't in the habit of becoming emotionally involved with her coworkers—present company excluded.

"I went to see a therapist, okay? I needed someone to listen, while I sorted things out."

"A therapist." He thought about that a moment, then slowly his hands started moving again.

Rae tried to relax, but the magic was gone. She wondered if Aidan could feel the new resistance in her muscles. She shifted higher on the cushion.

"Since you've deemed this to be true confession time, why don't you tell me why you really sent me to Pittsburgh? You know Harrison hired me to work on mergers and acquisitions. I thought I was doing a pretty good job there."

Aidan sighed. "You were terrific."

"So…?"

"Okay. Maybe I did have ulterior motives when I transferred you. But, Rae, could you really see us working together after what happened between us?"

Of course, she could. She'd imagined them together as a couple a hundred times before she'd slept with him. She'd seen them living together in a posh penthouse. Making love all night, then in the morning fighting over the business section of the paper before commuting to the office to grow their empire.

To her, it hadn't seemed much of a stretch. In fact, it had seemed like nirvana.

"What you're saying, Aidan, is that *you* couldn't see us working together."

"I couldn't see me working with you and not wanting you."

His frankness blew her away. She felt the heat of desire again, her hot, heavy need for him. "So?"

"You can't mix your personal life with your business, Rae. Surely you know that."

Yes, office affairs were always a mistake. Except for when they worked. She'd been so sure she and Aidan would work. But obviously, he hadn't seen their partnership as anything that serious.

"With me, business had to come first." His hands grew still as he explained. "Harrison and I have been friends forever. His father helped put me through Yale. Offered me my first job and the best opportunity I could have dreamed of. Do you think many men in their thirties get to run corporations of this size?"

Rae pulled her feet inward and sat up. "Your loyalty to the Kincaid family is admirable." But what about his loyalty to *her?* To the woman he'd slept with? Fathered a child with?

"It wasn't fair that you had to be the one to leave Seattle," Aidan said slowly. "But what choice did I have? I was the acting CEO, and the corporate headquarters are in Seattle."

"I guess it was just too bad for me that I was the expendable one." She almost felt guilty about the gibe when she saw how miserable Aidan looked.

Almost.

"You should have told me sooner how you felt about the transfer."

"Would you have listened?"

"I'd like to believe I would have." He eased off the sofa and headed for the window.

Rae watched as he leaned against the

window frame, his expression moody, brooding. He should have looked unattractive with that frown creasing his brow and his mouth tugging down at the corners. But he didn't. Damn it, he was the sexiest man she'd ever met. And he wasn't even trying to be. Which only made him more irresistible, as far as she was concerned.

With his fingers he combed his hair off his forehead, then turned to her with a grimace. "I should have resigned. That would have been the right thing to do."

"This isn't the nineteenth century. You didn't stain my honor or ruin my future, for God's sake. Just because I'm not thrilled about Pittsburgh doesn't mean I want you to resign."

He really must hate the idea of working with her if he'd even suggest that.

Boy, she'd read him wrong. She couldn't believe how wrong. She was usually skilled at judging people. Why hadn't she realized his feelings could be described as lust, just simple lust, and not...

Not what she felt for him.

Her throat got tight. Oh, no. She had to

think about something else. These days the smallest things…

She was having trouble breathing calmly. Damn! She didn't want to break down now, in front of Aidan. She needed to get out of this room and right away. She grasped the arm of the sofa for leverage, then swung her legs to the floor.

When Aidan realized she was trying to stand up, he moved quickly to help. His hands on the small of her back and her arm, were the last things she needed.

Eight months ago he'd made love to her so passionately—and yet tenderly, too. Even tonight, when he'd been massaging her feet, his hands had contained that same combination of strength and gentleness.

How could his touch feel so…caring… when his feelings weren't involved, at all?

"I'll make this right for you, Rae. I'll get you out of Pittsburgh. Name any city where we have business interests and I'll get you the best job possible."

For a smart man, he was so obtuse. He still thought this was about a city, about a job.

She felt the telling wetness in her eyes and averted her head.

"I—" Her voice wavered. She couldn't speak. What was the matter with her? Before all this, she'd never lost her composure so easily.

"Rae? Are you okay?" Aidan's expression shifted from concern to alarm. "Oh, no. You're *crying*."

She longed to refute him, but the first tear had broken free and she knew more were about to follow. *Damn!*

"Hormones," she muttered, and then fled to her bedroom.

CHAPTER TEN

AIDAN WANTED TO CALL Rae back, but what could he say to her? She was right. He'd treated her terribly. And yet, at the time, he'd felt he was doing what was best. What was right.

He heard the upstairs bathroom door slam. A moment later, the rush of water through the pipes of the old house indicated she was having a bath or a shower.

Her foot massage had been intended to calm and relax her. He'd achieved quite the opposite effect.

Turning to the window he saw a mirror-perfect reflection of himself. He tried to live so that he could look himself straight in the eye, with pride and self-respect. But tonight he had a hard time doing that.

It had been a long time since he'd done something that felt this wrong. Much as he tried to block out the memories, he found himself thinking of Simone and the other big mistake he wanted so desperately to forget.

Looking back, he knew he could have saved the situation by not inviting Simone into his house. But his mom had been dying and his guard was down.

"AIDAN? I NEED TO TALK to you. Something has happened." Simone's voice had been low, throaty, and her almond-shaped eyes were dewy with compassion.

He could have stepped onto the landing to talk to her. Instead, he'd opened the door wider.

She'd walked right up to him. Placed both hands on his chest. "Your mother just passed away. I'm so sorry, baby."

Aidan swallowed, remembering the pain those words had caused. He'd known his mother had only a little time left, but why did she have to die alone? He'd been at the hospice just hours ago and she hadn't seemed that bad. The nurses had told him to go home, get some rest and come back in the morning.

"No," he'd said to Simone. He'd tried to turn from her, but she'd held him tight.

Simone had comforted him.

And then she'd seduced him.

And in one night he'd lost his mother and betrayed his best friend. Aidan rubbed his face with his hands. After all these years you'd think the shame would ease, but it didn't. And now there was Rae.... He recalled the crumpled expression on her face in the seconds before she'd run from the room.

She could blame hormones if her pride required it, but in that moment he'd seen the truth. She wasn't just pissed off about the transfer. He'd hurt her.

Rae was so smart, so clever, so focused on her career, that he'd assumed it was all she cared about. In the months they'd worked together, she'd kept her emotions under such tight control that he'd almost come to believe she didn't have any.

Idiot.

Now with painful clarity, he saw the promotion to Pittsburgh in the way that she did, as nothing more than an attempt to buy her off. To get her out of sight, so he wouldn't have to deal with his own weakness.

The ceiling squeaked, and then a door shut firmly. Rae must have finished in the bathroom and gone to her room.

Aidan waited a minute, and then he went upstairs, too. As he'd expected, the door to Rae's bedroom was shut. As he passed the main bathroom, a waft of warm, humid air carried her scent. Across the hall the door to Autumn's bedroom was only partly closed.

Now that Harrison spent most of his time here on the island, Aidan didn't see as much of Autumn as he once had. He had to admit that was a relief.

It had been bitter punishment for his weakness when Simone and Harrison had announced they were expecting a baby just a few months after their wedding—and after Aidan's encounter with Simone. Aidan had never dared confront Simone about the dates, and consequently for all these years he'd lived with a constant reminder of his guilt.

Autumn.

Was she really Harrison's daughter? With all his heart and soul, Aidan prayed that she was. Every time he saw the little girl, he searched for signs of the Kincaid genes. Just his luck, the girl was the spitting image of her mother.

But it had seemed to him, the other day when he'd seen her on the beach, that she'd inherited Nessa's petite body structure.

Or was that just wishful thinking on his part?

He crossed the hall to Autumn's room, ostensibly to close the door. But he ended up peering inside. Autumn was still a little girl, and the patchwork quilt and yellow wallpaper reflected this. But he also saw evidence of her fascination with music. She had a guitar on her window seat, and a huge CD collection next to her stereo. He gave it a quick scan and saw every one of Simone's recordings.

Simone's presence in the rest of the house had been minimalized, probably out of deference to Justine's new position in the family. But here, several photographs of her remained. One on the night table had her standing with an infant Autumn in her arms.

Aidan couldn't resist. He went to the picture and picked it up for a closer look.

Simone's expression was dreamily maternal.

Her eyes, gazing almost, but not quite, into the camera, were just slightly out of focus.

What had she been thinking when that picture was taken?

He wished he knew. Would her thoughts in that instant give him the answer he craved? And if he had that answer, what would he do about it?

Aidan set down the picture and left the bedroom as he'd found it. If he gave Harrison his friendship and undivided loyalty for the rest of his life, he still could never atone for the wrong he'd done.

And now it seemed he'd injured Rae just as grievously.

"OUR STOCK IS UP two cents this morning." Rae kept her focus on the market listings, after she sensed Aidan's presence in the kitchen behind her.

Still, she felt Aidan's eyes on her for a long moment.

"The quarterly results came out yesterday," he said at last, matching her own casual tone. "I guess the market is impressed."

He crossed the room, sat down in the

chair to her right. He'd just showered and shaved and he looked good. Smelled good, too. She pushed her uncombed hair off her forehead, then passed him the business section of the *Globe*.

"Thanks," he said, glancing at her tentatively.

She lowered her eyes to her coffee cup, worried that he'd see the morning-after effects of the previous night's crying jag.

The crying jag she was doing her best to pretend had never happened.

Please don't say anything, Aidan.

"Is there any more coffee?" he asked.

"Yes. But it's decaf. If you want to make a pot of the real stuff, the beans are in the freezer."

He pushed himself up from his chair and went to the pot where he poured himself a cup. "I guess if you have to make do with this stuff, I can, too."

She kept her eyes on the paper. "I should apologize for my meltdown yesterday. I don't know what it is about pregnancy, but these hormones really mess with the mind."

Aidan sat down again. "Don't blame the hormones, Rae."

But she wanted to blame the hormones. She *needed* to blame the hormones.

He reached over and touched her cheek. It was a soft gesture, but she recoiled as if she'd been shocked.

"You had a right to be upset." His voice was as gentle as his hand had been on her skin. "I'm going to call Harrison later and suggest relocating you to Seattle. To head the mergers and acquisitions team."

She stared, not sure how to respond. He was offering her the dream job of her career. Eight months ago she would have whooped with delight. But now… "When this is over, I'm not sure I want to return to Kincaid Communications, Aidan."

"What?"

"It might be better for both of us if I didn't."

He looked dumbfounded. Then his jaw tightened. "If anyone is going to quit because of what happened, it ought to be me."

Not this again. "Don't be stupid."

"Why shouldn't I be the one to pay for my

mistakes?" He seemed to be asking the question of himself, more than of her.

"You've been friends with Harrison *forever*. You can't bail on him and his father's company. Just last night you were telling me how you owed him your loyalty."

"I owe you something, too."

"Well, I don't *want* you to quit! That's not what I want at all."

He threw up his hands. "Then, how can I make this right? Damn it, Rae. There has to be something I can do."

Love me. The words popped into her head out of nowhere. And in the next instant, she shut down that avenue of thought. "I don't need your help. I've got the situation under control."

He held her gaze steadily, then shook his head. "Bullshit."

"Okay, so I lost it yesterday. I'm better today. Really."

He didn't look convinced.

"Besides, there were two of us in that hotel bed as I recall. You can't shoulder all the blame for this pregnancy."

"I was your boss...."

"As I recall, I made the first move on you." They'd been eating a room-service dinner, going over the latest draft of the purchase agreement. He'd scratched out a clause that neither of them liked, and while his head was lowered over the papers, she'd reached across the table to put her hand over his. The next instant, they'd been kissing.

"Tell that to a judge."

"Oh, Aidan. Stop making this into such a big deal. As if I'm going to sue you for sexual harassment."

"Maybe you should."

"Now you're being ridiculous." She'd had enough. She downed the rest of her lukewarm coffee, then stood. "I'm going for a walk."

A beat later, Aidan said, "I'm coming with you."

The burst of joy she felt at his words frightened her. "I'm not sure that's a good idea."

Was it her imagination, or did he look a little deflated by her reaction?

"I'll do my best not to upset you. We can talk business. That's safe."

She pretended to consider his offer. The truth was, she craved his company too much to turn it down. "Well, I guess that would be okay."

"I'll grab the keys and meet you at the front door."

Rae ran upstairs to brush her hair and put on sunscreen. She was already in the tattered T-shirt and stretchy shorts she used for exercising. All she needed were her running shoes and sunglasses.

In the foyer, Aidan waited patiently. He had her wicker basket ready to go.

"I'm ready," she said, feeling a keen sense of anticipation. Normally she wasn't one for outdoor activity. She kept fit with regular half-hour trips to the gym, where she could maximize the efficiency of her workout with exercise machines and weights.

But since she'd arrived on the island, she'd come to appreciate the simpler pleasure of walking in the fresh air. In a gym, you never felt the brush of sea air against your cheek, or the warmth of sunshine like a comforting arm across your back.

"Another beautiful summer day." Aidan

inhaled deeply. "Being on the island makes me feel like a kid again."

Rae glanced at the house down the road, in the opposite direction from the beach. Several cars were parked in front of the pumpkin-colored saltbox bungalow. One of Molly Springfield's yoga classes must be in session.

Just as she thought that, a red-haired woman stepped out the front door. After the beautiful hair, the next thing Rae noticed was the lithe dancer's body.

God, she missed having a waistline.

The woman waved, and after a moment Rae realized she was signaling to them. Rae veered in her direction and Aidan followed.

The young woman ran toward them, still waving. "Hi, I'm Molly Springfield. I noticed you were staying in the Kincaid summerhouse." She turned to Aidan. "I think we met last summer."

"That's right. This is Rae Cordell. She works with Harrison and me at Kincaid Communications."

Molly held out a hand and gave Rae a friendly smile, which Rae did her best to return. The other woman's energy was a little overwhelming. "Your yoga studio seems very popular," she commented.

Molly beamed. "Yes, thank goodness. Coming here from Toronto was a bit of a risk, but everything has worked out fine."

"Summer Island must be a culture shock after a big city." Rae wondered why a young, unmarried woman such as Molly would make such a drastic move. They were about the same age, and she couldn't imagine living full-time in such a small, isolated area.

"I'm happy here," Molly said, offering no other explanation for the relocation. Her gaze ran unabashedly over Rae's pregnant figure. "You know, I have a class on Thursday mornings that would be just great for you. Are you having any back pain?"

Aidan frowned. "Rae's due in a matter of weeks. I don't think yoga is a very good idea."

"Oh, this is a gentle class," Molly assured them. She glanced at her watch, then made a face. "I really should be going. My next class starts in ten minutes."

She focused intently on Rae one last time.

"Think about that class," she urged. "No charge for the first one." She smiled again, then dashed back to her house.

Rae watched after her. "Maybe I should try yoga," she mused. "I'd love to have that much energy."

"You're fine the way you are." He cocked his head, studying her house. "I can't get used to all that color."

She considered the pumpkin-and-indigo combination. "I kind of like it."

"Well, maybe it's good she changed the house so drastically. This way I don't keep expecting to see my mom walk out the front door."

There was something tender in the way he said *mom*. As they began walking toward the beach she asked, "Were you close?"

"Very. She told me our family was small, but it was special. And it was, because she made it that way."

Rae felt the welling of an old sadness at his simple words. His mother sounded amazing. "How did she do that?"

"She was big on traditions. Not just for major holidays like Christmas, but little everyday things. Like in the morning she would make me breakfast and I would read her the important bits from the newspaper. Stuff like that."

Rae had never seen her mother in the morning before she went to school. "Did you ever fight?"

"Rarely. It sounds hokey, but my mom was so proud of me that I never wanted to let her down."

"Wow." She'd never fought with her mother, either, but for an entirely different reason. When it was obvious your parent could barely tolerate you, and when you knew that your mere existence had ruined your mother's life, well, there just wasn't much motivation for rebellion.

"My mom saw the bright side. Even when bad things happened."

Rae didn't think her mother had ever seen the bright side of anything. Except maybe a bottle of gin. "Were there a lot of bad things in your mother's life?"

His expression darkened. "My dad died in a skiing accident shortly after I was born. He was self-employed and had no insurance."

From the outside, Rae reflected, their situations were somewhat familiar. They'd both grown up without a father. Their mothers had both been forced to cope on their own. Was it possible her mother would have reacted differently—more positively—if her father had died, rather than left them on purpose? Somehow, Rae doubted that would have altered anything.

"Our life was just getting easier," Aidan continued. "Mom had been promoted at work and I was at a point where I could start helping her financially, as well, when the cancer happened."

"What kind was it?"

"Ovarian."

"That's tough."

"Yeah, it sure was. And not fair. Mom led such a healthy life. She ate well and exercised…." He shrugged. "I was pretty bitter about it for a long while."

Rae tried to imagine how it must feel to experience the untimely loss of a parent you had loved. When advanced liver disease had finally claimed her own mother, she'd felt nothing but relief. Maybe there'd been a little sadness there, but it had been more for what had never been than for what she'd lost.

"What about your mom?" Aidan asked. "How old were you when she died?"

"I was in university. She'd been sickly all her life. So it wasn't unexpected."

"Still, it must have been hard."

She said nothing.

"Rae?"

"Look, Aidan, I'd love to pretend that I adored my mother and was brokenhearted when she died. But I've already told you the truth about our relationship. It was terrible. Toxic. She brought out the worst in me and I guess I did the same to her."

"That's sad."

Now he was feeling sorry for her again and she absolutely did not want that. "I thought we were going to talk business?"

He was quiet. Then he sucked in a breath. "I had an e-mail from the office today. We got the usual terms on the acquisition line of credit from Chase Manhattan."

"Really?" She shook her head. "I think we can do better."

"I'm glad you said that, because so do I."

AT THE BEACH, they found two female volunteers sitting in lawn chairs next to a folding table. Expressions were grim all around, as Rae followed Aidan to the makeshift command post.

One of the volunteers, Maryann Simpson according to the badge she wore on her shirt, was about Rae's age. "I have three children of my own. This is just killing me."

"There's been no news?" Aidan asked.

"I'm afraid not." The other volunteer, Becky Stills, was older—in her fifties, at least. She showed them a detailed map of the area, marked in red squares. "Since he was reported missing, we've had search parties covering the entire southern half of the island. I just can't understand where he could be." Her gaze roamed out over the ocean and Rae guessed what she was thinking.

If Tyler had drowned, they might never find his body.

"I heard a helicopter earlier," Aidan said.

"Yes," the older woman said. "And the police are using search dogs, too."

"Is there any way we can help?" Rae asked.

Maryann glanced at Rae's belly and Rae

was certain she was going to tell her not to bother. Instead, the young mother passed her a clipboard. "Add your names here. We've got a full complement of volunteers, but if we need you, we'll call."

Aidan's name was already on the list, Rae noticed as she printed her own on the next available line. "Well, good luck," she said.

Both women nodded, but neither looked particularly hopeful.

Aidan took Rae's hand and led her down the beach, to an alcove created by several boulders. He spread out the blanket at their usual spot, then helped as she lowered herself onto it.

"Comfortable?" he asked.

"You're kidding, right?" She crossed her legs, making a nest for her belly. "Soon I'm going to need a crane to get up and down."

With a supple grace she envied, Aidan sank to the blanket next to her. "Not that much longer," he said.

Labor. She suppressed a shudder of fear, then closed her eyes to the prospect and tried to concentrate on the gentle warmth of the sun on her skin. When she next opened her eyes, Nessa and Autumn were walking along the boardwalk toward them.

They were holding hands, finishing off ice-cream cones and laughing. Rae felt inexplicably sad at the sight of them. She chased the feeling away with a smile and a wave. Nessa waved back.

"Nice day, isn't it?" Nessa said, when she was close enough for them to hear. "Autumn and I just walked to town and now we're going home to water the flowers."

Though her words were bright and cheery, her gaze took in the women at the command post and her smile faltered briefly. She didn't mention them, though, and Rae guessed she didn't want to discuss the missing boy in front of Autumn.

"That sounds like fun." Rae noticed Aidan's face had become tight and contained, as it had the last time they'd encountered Autumn on the beach.

"What about the piano, Auntie Nessa?" Autumn prodded.

"Oh, yes. We were wondering if Autumn could come by the summerhouse to practice the piano for a while this afternoon? Unfortunately there's no room for one at my place and Autumn's been suffering withdrawal."

"Piano." Aidan looked as if Nessa had mentioned a painful tooth extraction rather than a musical instrument. "Sure. If it's okay with you, Rae?"

"I'd love to hear Autumn play," Rae said, quite honestly. "Come by anytime."

She was curious about this little beauty, the daughter of a corporate mogul and a jazz superstar. Autumn had been polite and quiet each time she'd seen her, but there was a sparkle in her eyes that made Rae suspect the little girl didn't miss much.

"That's great, thanks. We'll come over around two. See you then." Nessa led her niece to her sporty convertible, bypassing the command post with plenty of room to spare.

Once they'd driven off, Rae checked out Aidan again. He seemed to be relaxing in the sun, his legs sprawled in front of him, his upper body supported by his arms as he tipped his face skyward.

"Is there a reason you didn't want Autumn to come by the summerhouse?" she finally asked.

His body tensed. He turned his head toward her. "Why do you say that?"

"I'm just wondering why Autumn makes you so uncomfortable."

His expression tightened still more. "Is it that obvious?"

"To me it is."

He said nothing for a long time, then he pointed to a circle of stones near the high-tide mark. "When we were kids we used to build a bonfire there most summer nights."

"You and Harrison and Jennifer?"

"Yeah. Plus Emerson and Gabe." He paused again. "And Simone."

He rarely talked about Simone's murder. Or Emerson's subsequent suicide a year later. It was the sort of sensational story you could never imagine happening to your own friends.

Yet the tragedy had left its mark on both Aidan and Jennifer, Rae realized. She had no idea about their other friend. Aidan never spoke about him, either. "Does Gabe still live on the island?"

"Sure. He owns the real estate company where Justine works, as well as the local newspaper."

"Are you planning to visit him while you're here?"

Aidan sighed. Scooped a handful of coarse sand and let it trickle between his fingers. "I'm not sure. We've kind of lost touch over the years. Especially since his marriage to Nessa fell apart."

He blamed Gabe for that, Rae surmised. "Is he a jerk?"

Aidan gave an unamused snort. "Probably no more than the rest of us. But he didn't treat Nessa well when they were married. He was blinded by his obsession for another woman."

"Simone?"

"Of course, Simone. Who else?"

Aidan sounded bitter. Extremely bitter. And suddenly the pieces fell into place for Rae and she saw the way it must have been for the gang on Summer Island all those years ago. Simone, hugely talented and glamorously beautiful, had been the flame, at the center of it all, while the others had been moths, competing for admission to the inner glow.

"Were you fixated on her, too?"

Rae was sure Aidan was going to tell her to mind her own business. He looked so angry and uncomfortable. But he took in a deep breath and gave her an answer she wasn't sure she wanted to hear.

"I tried not to be," he said. "I tried bloody hard not to be. But the more I kept my distance, the more Simone seemed to consider me a challenge."

Rae nodded. She'd known women like that. Women who were so used to men being at their beck and call that they went crazy when one resisted. "Did something happen between the two of you?"

"Once." Aidan looked miserable and ashamed. "Yeah, once it did."

CHAPTER ELEVEN

AIDAN WAS FINALLY talking. Opening his heart to her, the way she'd done with him that night in Philadelphia. Even though Rae wasn't sure she wanted to know the details of the story he was about to tell, she was moved that he trusted her enough to share it.

"When we found out my mom was sick, Simone opened a lot of doors for us. Money suddenly wasn't an obstacle, and her celebrity carried extra pull."

"Did that make a big difference?"

Aidan nodded. "The day after the diagnosis, Simone managed to get us an appointment at the Mayo Clinic. She hired a private jet...spared no expense."

"Wow."

"According to the doctors we saw there, it was already too late for any treatment to be effective. But Simone didn't give up. She got Mom an appointment with a renowned specialist in Boston. Unfortunately, he couldn't offer a better prognosis."

Even though many years had passed since his mother had died, Rae could see that it still caused Aidan pain to remember. "I'm sorry."

"Simone wasn't ready to admit defeat. She researched alternative treatments, found this guy with a herbal program in Mexico. But Mom didn't have the strength to pursue a cure at that point. And I couldn't blame her. She was tired and she was in a lot of pain."

"That must have been brutal to witness."

"It was. Simone found a wonderful hospice, more like a luxury spa than a nursing home. Mom was beyond caring at that point, but it made me feel better, knowing we were doing everything we could for her."

"How long was she there?"

"Only a few weeks. I'd taken leave from work and was spending most of my time with her. My biggest regret is that I'd gone home to shower and change when she died. I wasn't there." He clenched his jaw and gazed out at the ocean.

"So she was alone?"

He shook his head. "Simone was with her."

"Simone?" Rae couldn't picture the glamorous singer keeping a vigil by the bed of a dying woman.

"She was a complicated woman, Rae. She'd do something selfish and thoughtless, and you'd want to throttle her. The next minute, she'd do the most generous, kindhearted thing. She spent hours at my mother's bedside, singing quietly, sharing her stories of the rich and famous, sometimes just fetching ice shavings or painting my mom's nails."

Rae had never imagined the famous singer had this side to her.

"When my mother died, Simone came to tell me. It was late and we were both exhausted. I shouldn't have let her inside—I was always careful not to be alone with her. But she'd done so much to help us, and I guess I wasn't thinking straight."

Now Rae could see where this was headed. "That's when you slept with her?"

Aidan closed his eyes. Grimaced. "Yeah."

"Do you think she planned for it to happen?"

"It's more complicated than that. Simone

was always bothered by the fact that I didn't worship at her feet like most men. When my mother got sick, I think she saw it as her opportunity to finally win me over."

"That sounds so calculated."

"Yeah, at face value it does. But much as I hate to admit it, Simone wasn't all bad. She really did care about my mother. I know my mother felt that she did, anyway, and that counted for a lot with me at the time."

"What about the night your mother died? Do you think Simone came to your house expecting to sleep with you?"

"I honestly don't know. I'd like to give her the benefit of the doubt and say no. She was crying, and I don't think they were fake tears. We just started out hugging and somehow it changed between us."

Rae could tell he still felt awful about what had happened, and she wished she could comfort him. "The circumstances were highly emotional."

"Yeah, but she belonged to someone else. The wedding was just a few weeks away."

"*She* was engaged," Rae pointed out. "Not you."

"Maybe she made the first move, but I let it happen. Even though I was supposed to be the best man at her wedding."

The timing, Rae reflected, could hardly have been worse. "Does Harrison know?"

"God, no. He'd kill me. Gabe didn't make a secret of his feelings for Simone and Harrison hates the man."

"What a tangled web…"

Aidan cast her a cryptic glance. "It gets worse."

Worse than cheating with your best friend's fiancée? Rae's mind went blank, and then it hit her. Only one thing could possibly be worse. "How long ago were Simone and Harrison married?"

"Almost eight years."

"And Autumn is what…seven?"

Aidan gave her a twisted smile. "Exactly. She was born eight months after Harrison and Simone were married. As far as I can figure, it's entirely possible that I was the father."

PROMPTLY AT TWO O'CLOCK, Nessa and Autumn arrived at the summerhouse. Aidan had showered and changed since the excursion to the beach. Telling Rae his sordid secret had been easier than he'd expected. Still, it didn't make facing Autumn less painful. Every time he saw the little girl, his guilt nearly crushed him.

Harrison was his best friend. How could he have betrayed him in such an elemental way?

"Come on in." His voice sounded too jovial. Forced.

But Autumn made the moment easy for him, rushing for the grand in the rarely used front room, quickly settling on the polished wood bench seat.

Nessa looked at Aidan wryly. "My mother had to coax and bribe Harrison and me into practicing every day."

"Yeah, I remember." He ushered Nessa inside. "Rae's in the kitchen, experimenting with a deluxe juicer and a dozen lemons. Want to try her lemonade?"

"Sure. Thanks."

He followed Nessa to the kitchen, the sound of scales already reverberating in the open foyer. Autumn's efforts sounded much more professional than his earlier attempt.

"Hi, Nessa." Rae held up a glass of pale yellow liquid triumphantly. "I think I did it. Lemonade from scratch. Taste it, Aidan. Is it any good?"

He accepted the glass and sipped. It was too sweet and didn't have much of a lemon taste at all. "Yeah, it's good."

Rae frowned. "It is not. Give that back." She tasted, grimaced and spat it out. "I guess we'll be drinking plain ice water."

"That's fine with me," Nessa assured her.

They settled in the cushioned chairs on the back deck and Nessa chatted about her niece for a while. "I'm so glad Harrison and Justine agreed to let her spend a few weeks with me this summer. She's such a sweetheart, and I think it's good for them to have a little time as just a couple. Though I doubt they'll be 'just a couple' for much longer."

"Oh?" He'd wondered if they were going to have more kids. "Is Justine pregnant?" If anyone would know, it would be Nessa. She and Justine had been best friends since they were kids.

"Not telling," Nessa said coyly.

Which meant yes, of course.

"Wow. That's great."

"Please pass on my congratulations when the word is official," Rae added.

He wondered which of the two of them sounded the more stiff. Babies, especially the unborn kind, weren't exactly a comfortable topic around here these days. He decided it was a good time to broach a different subject.

"Is there any news about Tyler?" he asked.

Nessa's pleasant expression vanished. "Dex called at lunchtime. Still nothing. I'm trying not to focus on the negative, especially around Autumn, but every day that goes by, every hour, it's harder to hope...."

She shifted her gaze from him to Rae, tears making her dark eyes luminous. "He's such a sweet boy and he's faced so many difficult times in his life already. This is such a travesty."

"Have you seen his father again?" Rae asked.

"No, I've had Autumn with me, so I didn't have a chance to check in with him. But Dex did. He said Ted was still drinking late last night." Nessa shook her head. "That man is just hopeless."

"Does Dex think there's any chance his father might have hurt Tyler?" Aidan asked.

"I'm sure the possibility has occurred to him. But Jenkins has given him full access to the house and surrounding property. Dex and his men have searched the area thoroughly and haven't found anything suspicious."

Nessa made little circles with her glass, causing the ice cubes to clink against one another. "The kids in my before-school care program like to compare the lunches they bring from home. Poor Tyler always had the same thing. A cheese sandwich and an apple."

"Pretty basic," Aidan said.

"Yes. He never had homemade cookies or muffins like the other kids did. I remember one day his dad had thrown in a package of Smarties with the usual stuff. Tyler was so excited."

"Did he wolf down the candy as soon as he got to school?" Aidan remembered that was what he'd always done when his mother packed one of his favorite snacks in his lunch.

"He did open the box right away," Nessa

said. "Then he divided those little candies among all the kids at day care. I think he ended up with only three or four pieces for himself."

Nessa wiped a tear from the corner of her eye. "Every time I saw him, Ted Jenkins was such a grump. He was always impatient, snapping at Tyler to hurry, interrupting him when he tried to tell him about something that had happened at school that day. But to listen to Tyler talk about his dad, you'd have thought he was Bill Cosby and Fred Mac-Murray rolled into one."

Aidan noticed that Rae's eyes were looking a little bright now, too. "He sounds like a terrific kid."

"He *is*. I just hope so much that he'll be okay." Nessa stared into her glass, despondently.

Aidan guessed that she was thinking the same thing he was. Odds were, Tyler *wasn't* going to be okay. Not now that so much time had passed. What was even harder to endure was knowing they might never find out what happened to him. After all, children did disappear without a trace.

Aidan slipped into the kitchen and returned with a box of tissues. Nessa took one gratefully. Wiped her eyes and blew her nose. When he passed the box to Rae, though, she scowled at him.

"I'm not crying," she said, her tone unnecessarily defensive.

"Okay, you're not crying. But hypothetically speaking, say you were. What would be so terrible about that?"

He hadn't meant to make things worse. But Rae's face flooded with color at his words.

"I'm not an emotional person. I'm analytical and composed. Ask anyone I work with. I don't cry. Nothing makes me cry. Not even sad movies."

He placed the box of tissues on the opposite end of the table from her. "Calm down, Rae. I understand."

Her scowl deepened. "You understand? I don't think so." Turning to Nessa, she managed a short apology. "I'm sorry, but I need to go to my room for a minute."

And then she was gone.

He sat for a moment with Nessa, shifting

back and forth on the seat that had seemed so comfortable just a few minutes earlier.

Nessa looked at him solemnly. "She needs help."

"Yes."

"It isn't just her hormones that are making her so emotional."

He felt a bit like a wild horse, slowly being backed against a solid wooden fence. "I know."

"Well, Aidan. Do you care about her?"

"She's smart. She's beautiful. She's…hell. Yes. I care. I'm just not sure how much."

Nessa looked disappointed with his answer. "Figure it out, Aidan. That's your baby she's carrying." She paused. "I can't believe I'm doing this."

"What?"

"Giving you advice on your love life. I used to hate it when you and Harrison did that to me."

"You're talking about Gabe?"

"From the day I accepted his proposal, our relationship was under fire from you guys."

"We were just trying to protect you."

"Yes, well, in the end you were proved right."

Nessa looked at her hands, folded on the table. Aidan wondered if she was noting the absence of her wedding rings. Did she miss wearing them?

"If it's any comfort, Harrison and I would have rather been wrong."

She nodded. "You know what's so ironic?"

He waited.

"Once I told Gabe I wanted a divorce, he finally seemed to get over Simone."

"I heard he tried to convince you to give the marriage another try."

"Yes. And he kept trying until the day our divorce was finalized, about a month ago. I haven't heard from him since."

She sighed and he couldn't tell if the sigh was sad, or just resigned.

"Are you okay with that?"

"Yes, I am. I really am." She dragged her gaze up and looked at him solemnly. "Gabe is a good person. I know you and Harrison don't believe that, but he is. The day he signed our divorce papers, he told me if I ever needed anything to call him. And I know that I could.

"But I don't want to," she admitted. "I

wasted too many years in a dead relationship. But now…life is good. Or at least it was until Tyler went missing."

"I wish there was some way I could help."

"So do we all, Aidan. Right now the only thing that's giving me hope is the possibility that he's hiding from his father. That he found some safe place…" She stopped talking. Her eyes lit up. "I wonder…"

"What is it, Ness?"

"Do you think I could leave Autumn here for a bit? I probably won't be able to pry her from the piano for at least an hour."

Aidan didn't want to be left alone with Autumn. "Why? What's up?"

"I was just thinking about how Tyler loved to play in the tree house in my yard. Autumn and I haven't been back there all week."

"You think he could be hiding there?"

"It's worth checking."

Aidan agreed. "Should I call the police? Do you need help?"

"No. I'll get a hold of Dex if I find anything useful. Are you sure it's okay if I leave?"

"Go right ahead, Ness. I hope to God you find him."

RAE SAT ON THE FLOOR, her back pressed against the bed, and sobbed into her hands. She couldn't stop crying about poor little Tyler. The one time he got a treat in his school lunch, he'd shared it with all the other kids. She could just picture the smile on his face as he proudly doled out the little candies.

How many times had he watched the others eat their home-baked cookies and brownies while he had nothing? Had the others ever shared with *him?*

It was so unfair. He'd lost his mother when he was young. And his father was a drunk. And he was only a little boy and now he was lost, possibly *dead.*

And didn't it just prove that she was right to give up her baby? Because she couldn't even make a pitcher of lemonade, let alone cookies, and her child would have ended up like Tyler, with a hole in the place where a mother should be. As *she* had been when she was a little girl.

As she still *was.*

She'd never let anyone close before, but she'd taken a chance with Aidan because she'd thought, *Here's a man who gets me. He really gets me.*

And maybe he did, but that didn't make him love her. They'd had that one amazing night where she'd shared so many of the secrets inside her.

Then the next day he'd banished her from Seattle, from the office, from his side.

And now she was alone, the way she'd always been alone, the way she always would be alone....

She hiccupped on a sob, then sniffed. Her face was soaked. Her hands were dripping. Slowly, she worked her way up to her feet, then grabbed for the tissues on the bureau.

As she wiped away her tears, she gazed at the mirror and was shocked by what she saw. Red eyes, swollen lips, miserable expression.

Get a grip, Rae.

So what, that she'd had the bad luck to become pregnant by a man who didn't care about her. She wasn't a teenage victim. She was a healthy, well-educated, reasonably attractive, financially secure woman.

She had no business falling apart like this. She had to stop it. Pull herself together.

She blew her nose, brushed her hair, forced a smile.

The creature in the mirror grimaced back at her.

Get it together, Rae. Get it together.

She had to go downstairs and apologize to Nessa. She liked Harrison's younger sister. She was softer than Harrison, kind and considerate, but she had grit, too. Rae thought she was the kind of woman who would make a good friend.

She was just putting her hand out to the door, though, when a knock startled her from the other side.

"Rae?" It was Aidan. "Are you all right?"

She opened the door so quickly he almost fell inside. "Of course, I'm okay. Why wouldn't I be okay?"

She tilted her head back, gave him her most haughty look. If he noticed the signs of her crying bout—and how could he not?—he gave no sign.

"Nessa just left. She had an idea about where Tyler might have gone."

Tyler. Oh, please, let Nessa find him.

"Where?"

"I guess there's a tree house in her backyard, where he used to like to play."

"Brilliant." Rae could imagine a boy like Tyler hiding in a place like that. "I hope she finds him."

"Me, too."

"What about Autumn?" Rae could still hear the piano, louder now that she'd opened her door.

"Nessa's coming back for her."

"Okay." She waited for him to leave. But he didn't. Instead, he looked at her so tenderly, she had to glance away.

"Rae—" he started.

She couldn't let him finish. "I need to make a call," she lied, retreating to her room and closing the door firmly.

If she couldn't have Aidan's love, she wouldn't accept pity as a consolation prize.

CHAPTER TWELVE

NESSA LIKED TO THINK that her day care was a place where Tyler had felt safe and loved. And the tree house in her backyard was his most favorite place of all. Could he be hiding there?

It was a long shot, Nessa knew. Oyster Bay, where she lived and ran her child-care business, was almost three miles from Pebble Beach. Could a six-year-old boy walk that far?

She wasn't sure, but she knew she had to check.

As she drove toward her home, Nessa grew increasingly hopeful. Why hadn't she thought of this earlier? It seemed so obvious now.

She coasted her vehicle into her driveway, stopping the car with a jerk. Not bothering to grab the keys or close the door, she dashed for the yard.

Please, please, please, she prayed with each pounding of her footsteps. She stopped as she rounded the corner of the house. All was silent. The play center looked the same as usual.

"Tyler?"

She couldn't see anyone inside the tree house window. But he could be hiding.

"Tyler, come down here immediately!"

Nothing. Maybe he was frightened.

"I promise I won't be angry with you. If you're upset about something I'll try to help." Inspiration struck. "I have some cookies in the house. You must be terribly hungry."

Unless he'd been sneaking food from her kitchen? She wasn't very careful about keeping all her doors and windows locked.

Folding her arms over her chest, Nessa glanced up into the tree. If he was hiding, he was being very careful not to make a sound. The only way she could find out for sure, was to climb up and check for herself.

She assessed the rope ladder, uncertainly. She was wearing shorts and sturdy sandals. But her left leg had been weak lately. Would it give out on her if she tried to climb this thing?

"Please come down, Tyler."

As before, there was no response. Well, she had no choice, did she? Nessa grasped hold of the ladder with both hands, and took the first step. The ladder had been anchored at both top and bottom, so it didn't swing too badly. She climbed farther.

Finally, she was able to peer into the opening of the tree house. She was so convinced that she was going to find Tyler either sleeping, or crouched hiding in a corner, that she couldn't believe what she saw.

The tree house was empty.

And there were no signs that anyone had been inside recently, either.

Oh, Tyler. Where are you? She'd been so sure that her hunch was right. Now she felt bitterly disappointed. She lowered her right leg, searching for the rope below her. When her foot just swung in the air, she felt a moment of panic.

Why hadn't she remembered what she always warned the children? *It's easier to climb up than down.*

Nessa took a deep breath, gathering her strength. Her left leg, the one bearing most of her weight, had begun to tremble. She tried again to find the lower rung, but she didn't have the strength, didn't have the coordination.

This was stupid. Two years ago she'd have had no problem getting up and down from the tree house. Her assistant, Leslie, was older than she was, and Nessa had seen her climb up here a time or two to settle differences among the children.

Nessa wanted to keep trying, she *hated* to give up, but her trembling was getting worse and it was clear she'd have a better chance of success if she rested a little first.

So, she crawled up into the tree house and sat down. Five minutes later, she was almost ready to attempt the ladder again when she heard a vehicle pull up. A moment later, there was a loud knock on the front door.

She peered out the window. "Hello? I'm in the backyard!"

Less than a minute later, Dex's head appeared over the fence he had constructed several months before, for the play center.

His brown hair looked mussed and he needed a shave. She wondered how many hours he'd been working since he'd last had a decent night's sleep.

"Nessa?"

"Up here!"

He lifted his head, then his eyes rounded. "What are you doing in the tree house?"

For some reason his question annoyed her. "I'm playing. Isn't it obvious?"

"You left your keys in your car. I put them in your mailbox." He opened the gate, then slowly walked toward her. From his cautious expression, she guessed he wasn't sure how to interpret her remark.

"That tree house would have made a good hideout for Tyler." He took a roll of candies from his pocket and popped one into his mouth.

"That's what I thought, too." She glanced down at him, shaking her head when he offered the roll up to her. "But he isn't here."

"Too bad." He waited a moment. "So are you coming down?"

"Not yet."

"I see. I guess I'd better come up, then."

He grasped hold of the ladder, and a moment later he was sitting next to her, his head crouched. "I should have built cathedral ceilings in this thing."

She laughed. And suddenly it didn't seem like such a big deal that she'd gotten trapped up here. "An elevator would have been a nice touch, too."

"Still, it's kind of cozy, don't you think?"

They were sitting very close, Nessa realized. And the way Dex was looking at her, made it very difficult to breathe.

"Nessa?" He touched her hand and she felt a telltale shiver.

Why did it feel so right, being alone with Dex like this? They were squashed and uncomfortable. And yet...she didn't want to be anywhere else.

He moved his head toward her. He was going to kiss her. And she was surprised at how badly she wanted it to happen.

Ever since she'd left Gabe, she'd known that Dex wanted more than simple friendship from her. Of course, a romantic relationship was impossible.

And yet...

Their lips met and Nessa tasted coffee and breath mints. She realized she'd always associated the scent of peppermint with Dex.

He kissed her more deeply and she didn't notice flavors anymore. The world seemed to be spinning around her. She grabbed onto the collar of his shirt and held tight.

His arms wrapped around her waist and she felt the rough friction of his beard against her chin. Strangely, she found this arousing. Gabe had always been clean-shaven, even on holidays.

Nessa tried to pull Dex closer, but the cramped quarters frustrated her efforts. She heard his head bump against the roof and he sucked in his breath.

They stopped kissing and just looked at one another.

She wanted to tell him that this was impossible. He was a healthy, fit man. She had multiple sclerosis. He deserved better.

Instead, she thought about the hours he'd spent building this play center and the fence that kept the children from wandering too close to the sea. All the evenings he'd happened by the Cliffside Pub in time to join her for dinner.

He always seemed to know when she needed help. When she was lonely. Had he sensed, today, that she needed more than a friend? Was that why he'd climbed up this silly tree? Was that why he was kissing her right now?

"Oh, Nessa." He ran his hands down her arms. Kissed her again.

Her heart began thumping wildly. She couldn't stop her reaction, couldn't contain her feelings.

"Let's get out of here," she said.

Dex climbed down first, then held his hands up to guide her feet onto the rope steps. With his assistance, getting down from the tree house was no problem at all.

On the ground, he held her tightly for a moment, then pulled away. "I should get back to work."

"Yes." But it had been such a terrible week, she wanted his arms around her just a little longer. And looking into his weary eyes, it occurred to her that maybe Dex needed comfort, too.

"I know you need to go," she said. "But not right away."

She took his hand. Led him inside her house.

AT FOUR O'CLOCK in the afternoon, Rae was at the kitchen table working on a crossword puzzle, when Autumn came into the room, followed by Aidan.

"She's finished practicing," Aidan explained.

And Nessa still wasn't back. Rae exchanged a helpless glance at Aidan. How were they going to entertain the kid?

"So…" Rae forced a smile. "What would you like to do, Autumn?"

The little girl shrugged.

"Would you like a snack?" Aidan suggested.

Autumn considered the offer. "Do you have any cookies?"

He opened the pantry doors. "We've got crackers, chips…but no cookies."

"We could bake some." Autumn looked at Rae hopefully.

Bake. If anyone else had said this to her,

Rae would have been sure it was a cruel joke. She'd burned the bake-at-home loaf she'd brought from the grocery store. She couldn't even make lemonade.

But the earnest expression on Autumn's face was totally sincere.

"I don't cook, Autumn. I'm hopeless in the kitchen."

Autumn turned to Aidan.

"I've never made cookies in my life," he said.

"I have," Autumn said. "I can teach you."

Rae lowered her head over the puzzle. No way was she getting roped into this. Let Aidan deal with it.

"I'll give it a try," Aidan said, to his credit.

"It's not hard, at all. As long as you've got butter, eggs, flour and sugar."

"Flour and sugar," Aidan announced as he pulled the staples out of the pantry. He crossed the room to the fridge. "Eggs and butter are covered, too. Now what?"

"Okay. Next we wash our hands. That's what Aunt Nessa always does. Then we need to preheat the oven to 350 degrees."

Autumn put her hands on her hips as she

issued her orders. Rae, who was watching covertly, hid a smile. She'd always assumed that children were scary, irrational creatures. But Autumn seemed like a regular person. Only shorter.

Rae lowered her head and read the clue for forty-six across: "small pool." It was six letters and started with *p*. She filled in *puddle*.

At the same time, she kept an eye on the progress in the kitchen.

"First you melt the butter in the microwave, Uncle Aidan. Then mix in sugar and eggs."

"How much butter?"

"Hmm. I can't remember. I guess we need a recipe. Too bad we don't have any chocolate chips. There's a recipe on the bag."

"Here are some books." Aidan pulled down a tattered copy of *Joy of Cooking,* then lifted Autumn up onto the counter so she could read it, too. He ran his finger down the index. "Sugar cookies? Those sound good."

Autumn nodded. "I think that's the kind Aunt Nessa makes."

Rae continued to watch discreetly. This was

probably the first time Aidan had been around
Autumn without the protection of her parents
or her aunt. Rae could tell he was really
making an effort to get past his own issues.
When the time came, he would make a
great—

Don't go there, Rae.

She focused on the puzzle. The clue for
fourteen across read: "To crack, in a way."
Not eggs. That was for cookies. The word
that fit in the six-letter space was *decode*.
She penciled it in.

"Now we mix the flour and baking
powder and salt."

Autumn pulled out a second bowl. While
Aidan read measurements, she added each of
the ingredients, then stirred them together
and added them to the butter, sugar and egg
mixture they'd made already.

"Now we scoop the batter onto cookie
sheets."

Rae looked up, surprised. That was it?
That was all you needed to do to bake
cookies? She must have missed something
when she was concentrating on her puzzle.
Or even if she hadn't, she had no doubt that

if she attempted the same recipe she'd find some way to screw it up.

Ten minutes later, when Aidan was pulling the first tray of cookies from the oven, the doorbell rang. The door was unlocked and Nessa let herself in.

"Hi, I'm back," she called from the foyer. "Sorry I'm late."

"No problem. We're in the kitchen." Aidan lifted a cookie off the tray and raised his eyebrows at Autumn. "This looks pretty good, hey?"

Nessa entered the kitchen, stopping short in the doorway. Her cheeks were flushed and she tugged nervously at the hem of her T-shirt.

"Any luck?" Aidan asked.

"No. I'm afraid not." She forced a smile, probably for Autumn's sake. "I see you've been making cookies."

Aidan nodded. "Autumn taught me how."

He had a dusting of flour in his hair and a smear of batter on his T-shirt. Rae thought he looked cute.

"Can I take some home?" Autumn asked.

"They'll be too soft right now," Nessa said,

hurriedly. "How about you leave these for Aidan and Rae and we'll make some of our own tonight after dinner?"

Autumn looked crestfallen, but nodded.

Rae followed the group to the door to say goodbye. As Autumn gave Aidan a hug, Rae saw him slip the little girl a cookie shrouded in a paper towel.

"Come and play the piano whenever you want," he told her.

Nessa thanked them again, then left. As soon as the door closed, Aidan said, "Well, that was easier than I thought it would be."

He sounded pleased with himself. And Rae supposed he had reason to be. He'd kept Autumn entertained *and* he'd managed to bake something edible at the same time.

"What's wrong? Did I do something to make you mad?"

She couldn't answer him. Instinctively, she ran to her bedroom and closed the door. From out in the hall she could hear Aidan calling after her, but she ignored him.

Aidan was supposed to be like her. A business person. Career-oriented and goal-driven.

Yet he'd befriended Tyler Jenkins in one short hour on the beach. Despite having no previous experience in the kitchen, today he'd made cookies. He'd also managed to be kind to a child who reminded him of the time he'd betrayed his best friend.

She didn't want to admit it, hated to admit it, but the evidence was overwhelming. Aidan had terrific parent potential.

Oh, God, it was just so unfair.

THE NEXT MORNING Rae decided she wasn't up to her usual walk to the beach. She felt like visiting Annie, instead. When she shared her plan with Aidan, he insisted on driving her.

But being near Aidan didn't seem like a good idea. "You're supposed to be on vacation. Why don't you relax with a good book or something?"

"What if you go into labor while you're driving?"

She tried to ignore the panic sensation his words gave her. "Don't be ridiculous. Labor doesn't strike like a bolt of lightning. If I do start having contractions, I'll have hours to get to the clinic."

"What about all those babies born in the backseats of cars? I'm guessing sometimes babies don't follow the rules."

"I am not having this baby in the backseat of a car."

"No. Because I'm coming with you."

She couldn't argue anymore. Partly, she was tired from another lousy night with little sleep. And partly she admitted he might be right.

So she let him drive her. When they arrived, Jennifer was sitting on a bench on the front verandah, tying cut lavender into bunches. "I'll hang these from the rafters in the barn until they dry out," she explained, "then use them in flower arrangements and sachets."

Rae had never been one for crafts, and thought Jennifer could make far better use of her time playing the stock market. "Is your aunt around?"

"She's been spending a lot of time in her cottage lately." Jennifer frowned. "I think her arthritis is acting up, but she won't admit it."

Darn, Rae thought. She should have phoned ahead.

"Why don't you knock on her door, anyway?" Jennifer suggested. "I know she'll be disappointed if she hears you dropped in and didn't say hi."

"Thanks. I'll do that." Rae headed toward the cottage, leaving Aidan chatting with Jennifer. The other day Annie had told her she'd saved a memento from each and every birth she'd ever attended. Rae was curious about that collection. She wondered if she could convince Annie to show it to her.

Before she reached the cottage door, however, Annie came out and hurried toward her.

"Good. I was just going for a walk. Come with me and tell me how you're feeling. Have you been using the salve?"

Rae fell in beside the older woman, who was moving at quite a pace for someone with painful arthritis. "I have. It's amazing stuff. Very thick." Actually, the lanolin was so thick that it was hard to spread over her skin. But Rae tried every night. If Annie said it worked, she knew that it would.

"Good girl. You wait and see what your breasts look like when this is over." Wrinkles folded around her eyes as she peered closer at Rae's face. "Have you been sleeping?"

"I'm trying." Rae noticed that Jennifer had brought a tray of lemonade out to the porch. She and Aidan were now sitting on the stairs, each holding a glass and talking intently.

Probably Jennifer had made the lemonade from scratch, Rae thought bitterly, watching Aidan down his glass in several gulps.

She wondered if Aidan had ever been attracted to Jennifer, the way he'd been attracted to Simone. Jennifer was pretty, and she had a friendly, sunny personality. From the easy way they smiled and touched each other while they talked, they clearly enjoyed each other's company.

Rae tried to ignore the painful twist of jealousy that thought gave her. Aidan wasn't hers. She had no right to be possessive.

Besides, she'd come here on important business.

"Annie? Can I ask you something?" She stopped walking and clasped Annie's hands. The old woman's skin reminded her of rice pasta, thin and smooth. The joints in her fingers were hard swollen knobs. "I need to ask you a favor. It's a big one and I'll understand if you say no."

"Wait. Let me ask something first."

"Sure. What is it, Annie?"

Annie smiled slyly. "I want to be your labor coach."

Rae almost laughed with relief. "I guess you already knew what I wanted to ask."

"I was hoping," Annie admitted. "It's been so long since I've seen a baby born. My brother doesn't understand. He thinks I deserve a relaxing retirement, after all those years of being on call day and night. But I miss seeing a new life come into the world."

Rae blocked the part about the new life. The important thing here was that she wouldn't be alone. "You'll help me? Tell me what to do?"

"Yes, I will help. As much as I can. But you're going to be fine, Rae." They'd walked quite a distance from the house, but now Annie turned and looked back at the porch. "What about your man? He'll be there, too?"

Rae felt another painful twisting of her heart. "He's not my man. He's my boss." Annie deserved the whole story. "We made a mistake."

Annie's expression grew ferocious. "This baby is not a mistake."

No. Of course not. *She* was the mistake. The piece of the puzzle that just could not fit into the frame that nature had intended.

"Maybe you're right, Annie. But I'm giving up the baby after it's born. Don't forget that."

"I won't forget." Annie pulled her over to a cedar bench under the alcove created by a sprawling oak tree. "Now let me teach you how to breathe. This will be a big help when the baby comes."

CHAPTER THIRTEEN

ON THE DRIVE HOME from Lavender Farm, Rae couldn't stop talking about Jennifer's aunt. Aidan listened and quietly marveled at the fact that the other woman had made such an impact on Rae. He couldn't picture two more different women.

"She's seen so much. And she's so strong. Aidan, I've never met anyone like her."

He wasn't surprised by that. Where—in Rae's world—would she have met a woman like Annie March? "I'd have thought medical specialists and state-of-the-art hospitals would be more your style, Rae."

"Oh, I want both," she assured him. "But Annie has a lot of practical advice that doctors don't even think to give you. For instance, did you know that a woman is supposed to breathe differently depending on the stage of labor she's in?"

He felt like a complete neophyte. "There are stages to labor?"

"Well, of course. Aren't there stages to everything? It's sort of like a business acquisition."

"Come on, Rae." She had to be teasing him now. But her expression was serious.

"From what Annie told me, labor isn't that different from an acquisition negotiation. At the beginning you can't be sure if the process will be smooth or rocky. Sometimes everything comes together quickly, and other times the deal may stall. There may even be setbacks."

"Setbacks. I don't like the sound of that."

"Me, either. But serious problems are supposedly rare. Eventually you hit transition. The baby's coming out—like it or not. In an acquisition, this is when you perform your final due diligence and the deal is structured."

"And…?"

"Then it's pushing time. The baby is born. Your deal closes."

"Congratulations, ma'am. You're the proud shareholder of a brand-new corporation?"

"Exactly." Rae's voice suddenly lost its animation. She turned away from him slightly and he had to strain to hear the rest. "In my case, I'll only need bridge financing, since I'm passing ownership on to a different set of shareholders."

"Right," he said, as if there was no question about giving up the baby. But Rae had seemed so animated after her discussion with Annie that he'd wondered...actually hoped... she might have had second thoughts.

Just as he had.

He cleared his throat. "Rae, would you consider—?"

Rae started speaking at the same time. "Annie thinks I'm having a boy."

That derailed his thoughts. "What?"

"Annie thinks I'm having a boy."

A boy. Aidan was surprised at the immediate emotional impact caused by the idea of having a son. That was an age-old instinctive response, he supposed.

"Experts say you can't predict a baby's

sex without scientific tests," Rae said. "But I believe Annie."

She had her hands on her belly as she spoke, and Aidan realized it was something she'd begun to do more and more frequently. He liked seeing her cup her hands around the baby. It was something he'd like to do, too. Walk up behind her and wrap his arms around her waist, settle his hands on that firm, swollen belly…

"And here's the best part." Rae paused, for dramatic effect. "Annie agreed to be my labor coach."

He wasn't familiar with the term, but he had an idea of what it meant. "So she'll be in the delivery room with you?"

"Yes. Along with the doctor and nurse, of course."

"Well, that is great." A doctor *and* a midwife, that seemed like a smart combination. He waited for Rae to invite him, as well. Instead of feeling nervous about the prospect, he was actually excited. He imagined himself in that room…and when it was over, there'd be a baby. His son.

"I was expecting I'd be alone," Rae said.

"I never thought I'd find someone like Annie."

Aidan's fantasy abruptly collapsed. He realized he'd been foolish to think she might want to include him. Staying on in the Kincaid house and helping her through the last weeks of her pregnancy had been his idea, after all. Rae had made no secret of the fact she didn't want or need Aidan's help.

Suddenly the earlier question on his mind, whether she might be having second thoughts about adoption, seemed ridiculous. Good thing she'd interrupted him before he'd asked.

SEVERAL DAYS LATER, Rae awoke feeling restless and anxious. She was sick of drinking four glasses of milk every day, bored with the few clothes that still fit her, and most of all she was tired of having to lug around all the extra weight.

I want my body back! But that meant getting through labor, and despite the extra coaching she'd received from Annie, Rae most emphatically was not ready for that.

Which left her in a foul mood as she pushed herself away from the breakfast table.

"Time for my walk." She was going today, despite her lethargy. She couldn't sit at home and do crossword puzzles all day, as she'd done yesterday and the day before that.

Aidan had just put their dishes into the dishwasher. He dried his hands on a towel and said, "I'm coming, too."

She recognized that tone of voice now. "No sense arguing with you, I suppose?"

"None at all."

"That's what I thought." She sighed, but her exasperation was feigned. With each passing day Aidan was becoming increasingly protective and she was amazed at how much she liked it.

She, Rae Cordell, the most emancipated woman on the planet, enjoyed having a man take care of her. Not that she was ever going to admit it to Aidan's face.

"I'm tired of walking to the beach," she announced, once they were outside. "Let's go in the opposite direction, today."

"Sure. Whatever you want."

They headed west and after walking together quietly for a few moments Aidan said, "Did you have a chance to look over those terms on the line of credit?"

She was relieved he'd brought up business. Over the past few days they'd been going over a new plan together and she'd found the work-related distraction from her current predicament most welcome.

"Yes, I did," she told him. "I have a few ideas...."

They talked shop for half an hour before Rae realized that they'd reached the neighborhood she'd visited with Nessa last week.

"Let's take this road," she suggested, turning left toward the Jenkins house. As they headed inland, the houses became smaller, the yards less well landscaped than those along the more affluent coastal stretch. They passed a sign for Red Door Farms, and she remembered that that was where Jennifer bought her eggs.

"I'm not as familiar with this part of the island," Aidan said. "Looks like some of these homeowners aren't too house-proud."

He was walking so close to her now that occasionally she felt his arm brush against hers. "Nessa and I were here the other day. The Jenkins house is right over there."

She pointed toward a rusty mailbox, still tilted at an improbable angle. It was stuffed with mail, so much so that one letter was practically falling out.

"No kidding?" Aidan glanced curiously at the property.

The window blinds were closed. The truck Rae had seen in the drive a week ago was still parked there. She lifted the door to the jammed mailbox. The trapped letter fluttered to the ground. She stared at it for a moment, knowing she couldn't bend far enough to retrieve it.

As if reading her mind, Aidan scooped it up. "It's for Ted Jenkins, but it wasn't delivered by the post office. There's no stamp and no return address."

Rae felt a tingle of adrenaline in her nerve endings. "Maybe it has something to do with Tyler. Like a ransom note."

Even as she said the words, she was inclined to scoff at herself. Who did she think she was—Nancy Drew?

"I wonder how long it's been there?" Aidan said. "Obviously Jenkins hasn't picked up his mail for a while."

"It wasn't in the box the last time I was here. Nessa and I would have noticed." She held out a hand for the envelope, and when Aidan passed it to her, she examined it closely.

"It could be nothing, just a hand-delivered flier or something," Aidan speculated.

"Yes… But to be sure, we should get Ted to take a look at it."

"And the rest of the mail, as well." He gathered the mailbox contents into a bundle. "I guess we should try the front door."

"I hope he hasn't passed out already."

Aidan looked concerned by the possibility. "Maybe you should wait out here on the road."

And miss the good stuff? "No way. He isn't dangerous, Aidan." She thought about the bruises on Tyler's wrists. Okay, so maybe he had the potential to be dangerous. Still, last time she'd seen him, he'd been too drunk to stand, let alone hurt anyone.

They walked up the short approach to the house and Rae rapped loudly on the front door. She was surprised when it opened right away.

Though Ted Jenkins's eyes were bloodshot and he reeked of alcohol, he managed to speak coherently. "What do you want?"

His gaze traveled from Aidan to Rae. When he saw her he frowned. "I've seen you before, haven't I?"

"We met the day after Tyler disappeared. If you could characterize our encounter as a meeting."

"You were with Nessa Brooke."

"That's right. And you were drunk."

"Rae!"

Aidan moved a little closer to her. Whether to protect her, in case Ted took a wild swing, or to try and block her from view so that she'd shut up, Rae didn't know.

Ted was taking in more details now. He grabbed the letters in Aidan's hands. "What are you doing with my mail?"

Aidan passed it over—all except for the one piece that Rae still held in her hand.

"Your mailbox was overflowing," Rae explained. "We didn't want you to lose anything important."

"I don't get nothing important in the mail." As if to underscore the point, he tossed the contents of his mailbox onto the floor behind him, then tried to close the door. Aidan slid his shoulder into the door frame, however, in time to prevent this.

"Actually, there was one more thing." Rae held up the envelope, careful to keep it out of grabbing range.

Ted scowled. "What's that? Give it to me."

"This may have something to do with your son," Aidan said. And this time when he stepped closer to Tyler's father, it was clear that he was blocking Rae from potential harm. "Don't you think you should read it and make sure?"

Ted tried to reach for the letter, but Aidan stalled him.

"I could read it for you, if you like," Rae offered. Ted had not exactly been helpful in the effort to locate his missing son. If this letter did have information about Tyler, she didn't trust him to tell the police unless he was forced to.

"I'll bloody well read my own mail. Give it here."

Rae shrugged at Aidan. It had been worth a try. "Fine. Here."

Aidan took the letter from Rae, then stepped back, forcing Ted to leave the house and come out onto the steps. As soon as he did, Aidan moved between Ted and the door.

Smart move. Rae was impressed.

Ted Jenkins pulled a single sheet of white paper from the envelope. His fingers left dirty prints on the paper, as he unfolded it and read the message.

The paper was thin, and even from the back Rae could tell that there were only a few computer-printed lines. As he read them, Ted's scowl grew deeper.

He swore, then crumpled the page in his fist.

"Wait! Don't destroy that." Rae felt Aidan's hand circle around her arm, stopping her from trying to grab it. "The letter *is* about Tyler, isn't it?"

"It's just a bunch of damn lies."

"You should still show the RCMP," Aidan said. "You want them to find your son, don't you? I have my cell phone. I'll call them right now."

There wasn't much Ted could do about it, and he finally seemed to realize that. He opened his fist, took the paper and smoothed it out. Rae didn't expect him to let them read it and she was right.

She backed away from the front door and wandered to the side of the house. A rain barrel positioned under a downspout was full to the brim. She wondered if the water was ever used for anything. There seemed to be nothing planted or cultivated in the yard. Once there might have been a lawn, but now the yard was overgrown with indigenous grasses and weeds.

Less than ten minutes later, Dex pulled up in his cruiser.

"What's this?" Dex looked to Aidan for an explanation, but Rae was the one who answered.

"We were out for a walk when we noticed an envelope sticking out from his mailbox," she said.

Aidan had retrieved the envelope from the ground, where Ted had tossed it. He handed the envelope to Dex. Then Ted grudgingly passed over the sheet of paper.

It didn't take Dex as long to read the letter as it had taken Ted to do so. When he finished, he gave Tyler's father a long, sharply assessing look.

"Well, Ted," he finally said. "What do you have to say about this?"

"Nothin'. I don't got to say nothin'."

"You think it's a hoax?"

Ted Jenkins shrugged.

"What about the claim that you hurt your son?"

"That's all a pack o' lies! That's all it is." He turned abruptly, retreating into the house and slamming the door. The audible sliding of the dead bolt followed.

Rae leaned over to whisper in Aidan's ear. "He didn't even ask Dex if there was any news about his son!"

Dex must have heard her. "That man doesn't care about anyone but himself." He held out the letter so that Rae and Aidan could read it.

Mr. Jenkins, I have your son and he is quite safe. I saw what you did to him. Leave this island now, before I report you to the police.

NESSA FELT UNUSUALLY nervous as she watched Dex step out of his cruiser and head toward her. He had something in his hands, a clear plastic bag with a piece of paper inside. But she didn't focus on that at first.

She hadn't seen Dex since their afternoon together, and somehow he didn't look the same. He seemed taller, more handsome… sexier. She felt the heat rising in her face because of the way he was looking at her. She could tell he was thinking about their afternoon together, too.

She stopped pulling weeds from the flower border at the front of her house, and yanked off her gardening gloves. As she walked toward him, she was painfully aware of her slight limp. Though Dex's glance barely flickered, she knew he noticed it, too.

In that instant, she resented her disease more than she ever had since her diagnosis.

"Where's Autumn?" he asked.

"In the backyard, playing with a friend."

Dex made a move, as if to kiss her. She twisted her head, gave him a short, friendly hug, instead.

"Is everything okay?" he asked.

"Fine." She glanced at the bag he was carrying. "Is there any news about Tyler?"

"Yes. There's news. We found a letter."

She couldn't find her voice at first. "Is…is it a ransom note?"

"Not in the usual sense," Dex said, reassuring her. "Rae and Aidan noticed it sticking out of Ted Jenkins's mailbox this morning. I don't know how long it was in there. He hadn't picked up his mail in a while."

"Who's it from? What does it say?"

"It isn't signed, and I'm not sure what it means. I'd like to know what you think." Dex held out the clear plastic bag with the badly crinkled page inside, so that she could read the note.

As Nessa read the short typed paragraph, worry was replaced with hope. "But this is good. It means that Tyler is alive and he's with someone who cares about him."

"It could mean that," Dex replied. "Assuming the person who nabbed Tyler truly does have his best interests at heart."

"But it sounds like this person just wanted to rescue Tyler from his father."

"Maybe that's exactly what happened. But who? And did they have any other motive for taking this boy?"

Nessa realized he was thinking about sexual abuse. *Oh, please, no. Not that.*

"Really, this note doesn't tell us anything,

except to suggest that Ted was abusive to Tyler," Dex said. "And I think most of us already suspected that."

On a logical basis, Nessa knew Dex was right not to hold out too much hope. But she couldn't bear to think Tyler had been removed from one abusive situation simply to be landed in another.

"Dex, I've got to believe Tyler's alive and well." She glanced at the letter once more as Dex put away the plastic bag. "What happens now? Will you check for fingerprints?"

"The letter's been mishandled and I doubt we could lift anything from it, but we'll try. I have two officers making the rounds with the neighbors. I figure they're our most likely suspects at this stage. One of them might have heard Tyler crying and stepped outside to investigate."

"If they saw his father abuse Tyler, why wouldn't they have called the police?"

"Unfortunately, not everyone has faith in the system. There'd been efforts to get help for that family before, remember, and the problem wasn't getting better."

"That's true." She herself had tried to intervene and had accomplished little as a result of her efforts.

"We're also considering the possibility that someone driving by might have seen Tyler run out of the house and stopped to help," Dex continued. "There are a number of farmers who live farther down that road. We'll be checking with them, too."

Though he spoke with confidence, Nessa could see the doubt in his eyes. She couldn't let him give up. "You're going to find him, soon. I just know it."

He nodded, but not with much conviction.

She squeezed his shoulder. It must be so hard to be in his position. "You're doing a good job, Dex. No one could do more."

"Nightmares like this shouldn't happen on Summer Island."

"I know."

"There are other things, more positive things, I'd rather be concentrating on."

He looked deeply into her eyes, and she knew what he was referring to. But how could he want her, when her future was so uncertain? She'd seen the sympathy flash across his face when he'd noticed her limping.

Was that why he hung around? Did he think she needed him to take care of her?

"I'd better check on Autumn." She took a step away from him. "Thanks for stopping by. I'll see you later, Dex."

He put a hand on her arm to stop her. "Autumn's going back to Seattle soon, isn't she?"

"In a few days."

"Maybe we could go out to dinner next week. When all of this is over."

Did he think they'd have found Tyler by then? Nessa hoped so.

"Dinner would be nice, Dex. Let's meet at the Cliffside, as usual."

She saw the disappointment in his face, but she didn't regret the way she'd put that. She and Dexter Ulrich were better off staying friends, and one day he'd thank her for making this decision.

CHAPTER FOURTEEN

"MAYBE WE SHOULD HAVE accepted that lift from Dex, after all," Aidan said. Rae looked hot and tired, and from time to time she planted her palm on the small of her back.

"Why don't you stop here and rest? I'll go get the car and come back for you."

She scowled. "Give me a break, Aidan. I can see the house from here."

"It's still a quarter of a mile." They kept walking and a few minutes later one of Molly's yoga classes let out. A stream of people—mostly women of various ages, but a few men, too—headed for their parked cars and bicycles.

Last to emerge was Molly herself. She was engaged in an animated conversation with one of her students as she walked toward a light green VW. When she spotted Aidan and

Rae, she waved. The person in the Volks-
wagen drove off and she focused on them.

"Hi, there! You look tired," Molly said,
looking at Rae. "Would you like something
to drink?"

"I'm fine, thanks. We're almost home."
Rae spoke curtly, her eyes on the house
across the road. Her desire to keep moving
was so strong it was palpable.

Molly, being Molly, didn't take the hint
and back off. Instead, she started trying to
promote the benefits of yoga again.

"Rae, you really should try my Thursday
morning classes. They're gentle routines
meant for beginners, older people and those
with chronic health problems. Not that pregnancy is a problem, of course, but I think
some of the postures would help with your
back pain."

Rae removed her hand from the small of
her back. "I'm not the yoga type."

Aidan noticed Rae didn't even try to deny
that she was in pain.

Molly shrugged. "It's up to you. But you'd
be surprised how much it would help. You
know that boy who's missing? Tyler Jenkins?"

"Yes?" Rae said, and Aidan felt his own interest quicken.

"His mother had terrible back pain in the last stages of her cancer, and the yoga gave her some relief." Molly smiled. "Amanda wasn't the yoga type, either."

"What type was she?" Aidan couldn't help but be curious.

"Hardworking. Quiet. It took some doing to convince her to try yoga, too. She was too busy working at the grocery store in town and looking after her husband and her son."

"Was she a good mother?" Rae asked.

"I'd say yes, but I didn't get a chance to know her that well. She'd only been in my class a few weeks when the cancer advanced and she became bedridden. One of the last things she said to me was that she wished she had a sister or a mother on the island. Someone to make sure Tyler would be okay once she was gone."

"Was she worried about leaving her husband alone with Tyler?" Rae asked.

"At the time the idea didn't even occur to me. I just thought she wanted someone with a woman's touch, you know? But lately I've been hearing rumors that make me wonder."

"Rumors about Ted Jenkins?"

"Yes. Mostly about his drinking. But some are saying that maybe he did something to his son." Molly shivered. "Possibly even killed him."

An oncoming car signaled, then pulled over to the side of the road. A moment later, a woman on a bicycle came into view.

"Looks like my next class is starting to arrive." Molly glanced at Rae once more. "My offer stands, if you change your mind about the yoga. You can sit in on the first session for free."

"Gee, thanks," Rae muttered, as the lithe woman moved out of sight. "I can barely move from a standing position to a sitting one, and she wants me to do yoga."

Aidan knew better than to argue, even though he figured the yoga might be worth a try. "Don't you have a doctor's appointment today?"

"At two." Rae did not sound happy about it.

"How about I make you some lunch, and

then drive you?" To his surprise, Rae didn't argue.

"Do you think Molly could be right, that Ted killed Tyler? He could have typed that note and stuck it in his own mailbox to divert suspicion."

"It's a possibility," Aidan conceded, as they walked up the porch steps together. "But I'd rather believe Tyler was abducted."

"Yes," Rae agreed.

At least that way there was a chance the boy was still alive.

FINALLY HOME, in her bedroom, Rae kicked off her sandals. She fell back onto the bed, resolving to sleep until it was time to leave for the appointment.

An hour later, Aidan woke her with a lunch tray. He'd grilled a cheese sandwich and tossed fresh tomatoes with olive oil and herbs for a salad.

When she'd eaten, he helped her into the passenger side of his low-slung sports car. "Whoever designed this thing obviously knows nothing about being pregnant," she muttered.

She felt a little guilty for complaining. Aidan was being so attentive. He'd even helped her squeeze her feet back into her sandals before she left the house.

At the clinic Dr. Marshall wanted to perform an internal exam, so Aidan left Rae alone to change. Rae hated the stiff blue gown with the ties at the back. She sat on the paper-covered examining table with her bare butt exposed and thought, how demeaning! Then she swung her feet out and stared with disgust at her swollen toes.

Before she'd become pregnant she hadn't even known that toes could swell.

She hoped the doctor didn't suggest another foot massage to Aidan. The last one had been an absolute disaster. Though it had started out pretty nicely…

There was a tap on the door. "Can I come in?"

Dr. Marshall stepped inside and set about checking all sorts of things—including Rae's cervix—that Rae didn't want to think about. Rae distracted herself by counting the specks on the ceiling tiles.

"Okay, Rae. You can sit up now."

"That's easy for you to say."

Dr. Marshall laughed and held out a hand to help her, before inviting Aidan into the room. Accompanying him was a nurse who arrived to check Rae's blood pressure. Gee, was there anyone else in the reception area who might want to join them?

Rae clamped her teeth together, to hold the negative comments inside. She didn't want to antagonize the doctor, since Elizabeth Marshall had the power to authorize pain relief when it came time for Rae's delivery.

Rae felt her stomach clench with anxiety.

Oh, God. Only two weeks.

And then Dr. Marshall made it worse. "The baby's head has dropped into the birth canal, Rae. And your cervix is slightly dilated already. You could go into labor at any time now."

"But I have two weeks to go!"

"Babies aren't known for keeping to a rigid schedule."

"But I'm not ready," Rae insisted, knowing that what she said didn't make any sense. She didn't want to be pregnant a day more than necessary. And it wasn't as if she needed more time to kit out a nursery or buy a car seat or any of that stuff.

Aidan took her hand. "You're just nervous. But it's okay, Rae. You're going to be fine."

"How do you know?"

"Because I know you, Rae. You can do anything you set your mind to."

It was such a nice thing to say and just like that she went from feeling as prickly and angry as a stock trader in a bull market, to as sentimental and weepy as a greeting card.

Aidan was looking at her as if she was the most amazing woman in the world, and Rae just didn't know if she could stand it. She blinked away the unwanted tears in her eyes as the nurse attached the blood pressure cuff to her upper arm.

The doctor must have been struck by Aidan's comment, too, because she said, "And do you still intend to go through with the adoption process?"

That snapped Rae's mood back into line quickly. "Of course."

The doctor's eyebrows went up and so did the nurse's. Aidan looked as if he was going to say something, but instead, he moved back near the door and crossed his arms over his chest.

Rae should have been used to being judged for her lack of maternal instincts, but for some reason the obvious disapproval really rankled today. "I suppose you think I'm a terrible person?" she said to the doctor.

Dr. Marshall's expression became neutral. "Not at all. I wish more mothers who weren't capable of looking after their children took that route. I saw many abused and neglected children when I worked in the E.R. in Vancouver, and it used to break my heart.

"Not that I'm accusing you of being that sort of person," she added.

Gee, thanks, Rae almost said. But then she wondered if those children were the reason the doctor had decided to relocate and take up a quiet medical practice on Summer Island?

"Blood pressure is 120 over 80. Perfectly normal." The nurse removed the cuff and left the room.

"You're a healthy woman, Rae, and your baby is still active, with a strong heart rate."

"That's good to hear." Aidan smiled at Rae and she found herself smiling back.

"Just take things easy and I'll see you both next week." Dr. Marshall pulled off her latex gloves. "Unless I see you sooner."

AIDAN COULDN'T TALK for a while after the appointment. Thankfully, Rae seemed to be in a reflective mood, as well. She didn't say anything when he took the eastern road out of town, heading in the opposite direction from their temporary home.

The elevation was higher on this side of the island. Perched on one of the cliffs was a sleek, modern structure, all glass and gray cedar.

"What's that?" Rae asked. "A museum?"

The house really was the grandest building on the island. "No. Gabe Brooke lives there."

"He's the Forget-Me-Not friend you don't talk to anymore, right?"

"Right." Aidan felt a little guilty about that. Once they'd been such close buddies. He'd always admired Gabe, maybe even been a little jealous of him. It was hard not to envy Gabe. Good-looking, athletic, charming—he'd been born with all the advantages.

And with loads of confidence to match.

All his life, he'd gotten what he wanted. No wonder he'd been so flummoxed when Simone had chosen Harrison over him. But why had he then married Nessa, knowing he loved another woman? That was the mistake that neither Aidan nor Harrison could manage to forgive.

"You still blame him for hurting Nessa?"

"She's like a sister to me, Rae. I can't help feeling protective toward her."

"Does she still love Gabe?"

"I don't think so. She's got someone new in her life now."

"The Mountie? Dex Ulrich?"

Of course, she'd noticed, too. "Yeah, Dex." He pulled into a roadside rest stop that offered a spectacular view of the bay below. On the horizon you could just make out the profile of Saltspring Island.

Aidan got out of the car and went round to the passenger side. Rae didn't question what they were doing. She let him lead her down a short path, to a bench hidden from view by a bramble of blackberries.

"It's pretty here."

Rae was looking at the view, but Aidan was more interested in her. The feelings he'd been having at the doctor's office flooded over him again.

Pregnant women weren't particularly beautiful, or at least he'd never found them so. But this afternoon, watching Rae perched nervously on the examining table, he'd found himself thinking that she was the most stunning woman he'd ever seen.

Now that he didn't have to concentrate on the road, he couldn't take his eyes off her.

He let his gaze drop to her belly. She didn't like him looking at her there, he knew, but he couldn't resist. "Can I touch?"

He expected a sarcastic rejoinder, but she amazed him by lifting her T-shirt and exposing bare skin.

Slowly, he reached out a hand and let it gently rest on the curve of her belly. As before, he was startled at the firmness of it. The silky softness of the skin. He let his hand glide down the slope, then to the side. He couldn't feel any movement. The baby was sleeping.

Rae closed her eyes, leaving him guessing

about her thoughts. Did she mind him touching her like this? At least she didn't slap his hand away. Her thick, dark lashes lay softly against her pale skin. Her lips were lush and slightly parted. No doubt about it. She *was* beautiful.

With his hand still resting on her belly, he kissed her.

At the first touch of his lips, her eyes flew open. A moment later, she closed them again. He kept kissing her, placing his arm behind her neck, so she could lean back. As she let her weight drop onto him, he felt a surging of emotion again, a fierce desire to protect her and hold her and take care of her.

His touch grew more possessive, as he caressed her belly, over and over. Inside was a baby, *his* baby, and it had never felt more real to him than it did right now. His hands slid up her stomach, just under her breasts. He waited for her to protest, but when she said nothing he let himself explore further.

Her bra was industrial-strength, and it strained with the weight of her voluptuous breasts. Through the thick fabric, he caressed one breast and then the other, all the time feeling himself sinking deeper and deeper into the sweetness of this moment.

He wanted to tell Rae she was astounding. That what was happening to her body was a miracle. He wanted to strip off her clothes and examine every inch of her beautiful pregnant body.

Instead, he pulled himself together, gentled his touch to the merest of brushes, and finally stopped touching her altogether. He pulled her T-shirt back over her belly.

Rae drew in a ragged breath. "What the hell was that?"

Her eyes were luminous as they focused on him. So luminous he couldn't take offense at her words.

"I'm not sure," he admitted. "But it felt pretty amazing."

"You get off kissing pregnant women?"

"I get off kissing *you*. Pregnant or not." As he spoke the words, he was surprised that he hadn't understood this before. Rae was *it*. The one he wanted. He'd recognized that about her the first time he'd kissed her. Make that the first time he'd met her.

Instead of embracing the discovery—he'd

run from it. He'd sent her to Pittsburgh rather than deal with his own emotions. Rather than take a chance on their future. Just as he'd tried to run from Simone. In her case, his response had been right. His friendship with Harrison hadn't been worth losing over the love of a woman.

But Rae was different. She didn't belong to anyone else.

Except me.

"Rae—"

"God, my back is killing me." Rae moved deftly out of his arms. She put her hands on her lower back and arched gently. "I think I'll send David Letterman a list of ten things a nine-months-pregnant woman should avoid. Top of the list will be necking on a park bench."

She was making light of their experience. But Aidan was sure she'd been into it earlier. They needed to talk about this. What had happened and what it meant.

"Rae?"

She must have discerned the serious note in his voice because her tone grew cautious. "Yeah?"

"Do you think we'd have a chance, if we took the traditional route with this?"

"You mean using a bed instead of a park bench?"

"I mean getting married and keeping the baby."

Her eyes shot open wide.

Worried she might lose her balance on the uneven ground, he put his arm around her back. She'd started to tremble. Hell, he should have eased into this conversation gradually, not sprung his plan on her cold.

Maybe if he presented it like a business opportunity, she'd be more receptive. "Think about it, Rae. Logically."

She gazed at him, still mute.

"We're attracted to each other, right? And we've got interests in common. That's a pretty good start." He searched her face, her eyes, looking for a spark of connection that would tell him they were on the same page.

Nothing. She gave him nothing.

"Do you understand what I'm saying, Rae?"

She took a step back. "You want to keep the baby."

"Well…yes."

She lifted her hand and he watched in utter amazement as she almost smacked him with it. He caught her wrist at just the right time.

"Rae?"

"You bastard," she said. Then she headed for the car.

CHAPTER FIFTEEN

RAE HATED THE FACT that she needed Aidan's help to get back into the car. She avoided looking at him when he offered her his hand, but she had to take it. As she settled back on the leather upholstery, her legs were trembling.

Without a word, Aidan climbed into the driver's seat and took off. As he headed toward home, Rae kept her head angled to the right. The scenery passed in a blur.

She couldn't believe she'd let him get to her like that. Where was her backbone? Her self-respect? She'd just *melted* when he'd started kissing and touching her. He could have done *anything* to her and she would have let him.

And he'd just been manipulating her. Softening her up so he could spring that damn proposition on her.

What a jerk.

"Look." Aidan's voice was terse. "I don't know why you're so angry. A guy doesn't expect to get slapped just because he's asked a woman to marry him."

"Oh, really? Before you knew I was pregnant, you couldn't put enough miles between us. Now you're suddenly talking about how compatible we are. Don't you think I see through all this?"

Aidan's jaw tightened. "That was a sincere proposal."

"Yeah, I know. You sincerely want this baby. You're willing to marry me to get it. Well, guess what? I'm not going to use this innocent child that way."

"I am not *using* our baby."

"Oh. So if I hadn't gotten pregnant, you still would have asked me to marry you."

No answer. Rae squeezed her hands into fists. Sincere proposal. Yeah, right.

"Look Rae, we can't change the situation. All we can do is deal with it. And I think that marriage ought to be an option. We should at least *consider* it."

"You don't get it, do you? I'm not mommy

material." How could she convince him? "I've already told you about my mother. You know what my childhood was like. Do you want that for this baby?"

"It doesn't have to be that way. It *wouldn't* be that way."

"Our situations aren't as different as you think. My mom 'had' to get married, too, you know. And it was a huge mistake. Her rich, high-society family cut off all contact with her. Then, to top off her misery, a few months after I was born, her husband left her."

"If I marry you, I won't leave you."

Rae could feel the sincerity behind his promise. And it scared her. Aidan was just the type to stay in an unhappy union out of a sense of responsibility. It was up to her to make sure he didn't put himself in that situation.

"When I was little, I used to wish that my mother had put me up for adoption. I would have been happier. I think we both would have been happier."

Aidan looked incredulous. "You aren't serious?"

"Oh, but I am. The great thing about adoptive parents is that they really, really have to want a child. Don't you think our baby should have that? The gift of knowing that he or she is genuinely loved, by good people who know how to be parents."

Aidan's hands tightened on the wheel. "Like Julia and Neil Thompson?"

Just hearing their names made her heart ache. "That's right."

"I read that dossier you gave me."

She waited. "And? Did you find anything wrong with them?"

"They sound fine on paper. But have you met them?"

God. She squeezed her eyes shut. As if she could stand *that*. "I'm not only relying on the information the adoption agency gathered. I hired my own investigator. She was very thorough. These are good people."

"I'm sure the Thompsons would make great parents. The only thing is—that's our kid inside you, Rae. *Ours*. Doesn't that mean anything to you?"

She hated him, Rae decided. She really, really hated him. Didn't he understand that it was because she cared so much, that she'd chosen this route?

278 A BABY BETWEEN THEM

"I can't be a mother. So don't ask me to marry you again for the sake of the baby. It isn't the right thing to do. It never is."

NESSA PEERED DOWN at her niece, sleeping peacefully on the bed in her guest room. Her parents were arriving on the island tomorrow. Harrison and Justine planned to spend the night here with her, then drive back to Seattle the next day with their daughter.

Nessa kissed Autumn's warm pink cheek. She was going to miss her.

If only I had a daughter of my own. Or a son...

The bitter longing didn't feel as raw as it once had. Over the past year she'd come to terms with the reality of her loveless, childless marriage and the six years she'd spent with Gabe. The failure of that marriage was a loss she had to accept, much as she had to accept the MS. At least, in the end, she'd had the courage to seek a divorce and move on with her life.

And she was still young. Justine kept telling her she could have a half dozen kids still, if she wanted to. And Nessa knew that was true. The MS wouldn't stop her from having babies, though some of her symptoms might be affected when she was pregnant.

Still, deep her in heart, she figured children were not going to be part of her future. Not children of her own.

Nessa headed for the living room. It was past midnight, but she didn't want to go to bed. She knew she wouldn't sleep. Tyler had been missing for almost two weeks now.

Where was he? Was he cold? Hungry? Hurting…or worse?

She couldn't stand to imagine what he might be going through. And yet she couldn't completely put the possibilities out of her mind, either.

She settled on the couch with a heating pad on her sore leg. If she wanted to get her symptoms under control, she'd need to relax. Easy to say; not so easy to do.

She reached for the remote control to the TV, then paused as she heard a vehicle pull up outside her house. Suddenly alert, she went to the front door and checked the peephole.

Dex was standing on her porch. She was

so glad to see him, but she held back on the urge to throw herself into his arms. She didn't have that right. Besides, he looked exhausted.

And demoralized.

She didn't need to ask to know there'd been no breaks in the search for Tyler.

"I saw your light as I was driving past. Are you okay?"

She nodded. Poor Dex. Working until all hours, then checking in on her when he should be home in bed. "Have you eaten?"

He scratched the side of his neck. "Can't remember."

Without another word, she led him to the kitchen. She made a sandwich from leftover grilled chicken and brewed him a cup of tea.

He ate like a starving man. "This tastes great, Ness."

She cut a piece of blueberry pie, then sat across the table from him and watched. When he was done eating, she covered his hand with hers. "You're doing the best you can."

"It's not good enough."

"Oh, Dex." She knew he felt sick about Tyler, and so did she. Why did innocent children have to suffer in this world?

"We've talked to all the neighbors. The farmers farther down the road... No one admits to knowing about any problems in the Jenkins household on the night Tyler disappeared."

"Can I see the letter once more? Do you still have it?"

"The original's in the office. But I have a copy." Dex pulled a sheet of paper from his shirt pocket and passed it to her.

She read the short note again, and then sighed. "I want so badly to believe that whoever wrote this truly does have Tyler's best interests at heart."

"I do, too. But you know it's possible Ted typed this himself. He doesn't have a computer at home, but he could have used the one at the library. Emma says he was in there four days ago, supposedly returning some books of Tyler's, but she saw him at the computer for at least an hour."

Discouragement rose again. "I see. You think he typed this letter to divert suspicion from himself?" And there was only one reason Ted would have done that: because he'd killed his son.

"It's possible. But it's equally possible that someone else really did take Tyler."

Please, let that be the answer. "If so, at least they don't want money."

"If this was about money, Tyler would have been the last child on the island to be abducted."

Nessa had to agree. "Especially since Ted is currently unemployed."

"As it happens, I talked to Ted's former employer today."

"Didn't he work at Sam Olsen's fishing operation?" Nessa knew Sam. He played tennis with Gabe. He was a good man, strong-minded and yet fair.

"Sam says he had to let Ted go because he was drinking on the job. When he gave him the pink slip, Ted took a swing at him. Nearly broke his nose."

Sam was a quiet man, but tall and strong. If he'd wanted, he could have made mince-meat out of the smaller man. "Did Sam press charges?"

"No. He said he figured Ted had enough trouble."

"Sam's a good guy." Nessa rested her chin on her hand. "And he's right. Ted has had a rough couple of years."

"Yeah." Dex looked at her bleakly. Then he seemed to snap out of his troubling thoughts and focus on her. "But this isn't good late-night conversation. You should be relaxing. Sleeping."

She didn't say anything.

Dex's voice softened. "I know it's hard, but you have to try not to worry so much. Worrying doesn't help."

"Days are easier. Autumn keeps me busy. I'm going to miss her when she leaves tomorrow."

"Her parents picking her up?"

Nessa nodded. "They're coming in on the morning ferry."

Dex rose, carrying his empty plate and fork to the dishwasher. "I should let you get some rest."

She didn't want rest. Didn't want him to go. Still, she got up from the table, too, and followed him to the front door, keeping behind him so he wouldn't notice her limp.

At the door he paused and looked at her intently. "You take care, Nessa."

"You, too, Dex."

The moment dragged on. She could feel his need to kiss her and it took all her willpower not to throw her arms around his neck. Deliberately, she took a step backward. Dex blinked, then his chest expanded as he inhaled deeply.

"Lock the door after me," he said.

"I will."

He looked as if he was about to say something else, but instead he just nodded, then turned and left.

She engaged the dead bolt, waiting until she'd heard him drive off to turn out the porch light. Dex had enough to worry about without adding her welfare to the list. Rather than checking on her, he should have been home catching up on the sleep he so desperately needed.

She pulled the curtains tight and turned out all the interior lights except for one in the hallway. Then she returned to the couch, to her heating pad and the waiting television. Tonight she couldn't bear to crawl into her queen-size bed alone.

AROUND TWO IN THE MORNING Aidan got over being angry at Rae. He was in the second-floor turret room, prone on the couch, flicking channels on the TV. When Simone had lived here, this space had been her studio. Now it was equipped with an entertainment center, a Ping-Pong table, another smaller table for crafts, games and puzzles, and a big, comfy corduroy couch.

Aidan clicked off the television and stared at the ceiling. Tired yet restless at the same time, he kept shifting positions, unable to get comfortable even though the couch was soft and inviting.

He'd never proposed to a woman before. So maybe he hadn't done the smoothest job of it. Still, he didn't think he'd deserved to be called a *bastard* because of it.

A simple "no" would have been easier to handle.

Or would it?

He couldn't stop thinking about how sweet

it had been to kiss Rae again. And how unbelievably erotic her pregnant body had felt under his touch. His physical need to be near her tonight was almost unbearable. Worse, was his emotional craving for her company, which she'd denied him by taking her dinner up to her bedroom and staying there all evening.

Wasn't proposing marriage the honorable thing to do in this situation? He wouldn't have done it if he didn't think he could offer Rae and the baby everything they needed. Including love.

In the morning, he'd talk to her again. Explain that he hadn't been talking about a marriage of convenience. She'd apologize and everything would get sorted out, eventually...

Having negotiated a compromise—at least in his own mind—Aidan drifted off to sleep. When he next opened his eyes, sunlight was glowing through the three-sided turret window. He checked the time on his wristwatch. Past ten. Wow, he hadn't slept so late in years.

Downstairs, he found a note from Rae. "Gone shopping."

He went to the living room and checked out the front window. Her rental car was gone.

He returned to the kitchen to brew coffee, grabbing the real stuff from the freezer since Rae wasn't around.

If she was shopping, she wouldn't be gone long, he reasoned. There weren't enough stores on the island to keep her occupied for more than an hour. Possibly two, if she decided to stock up on groceries.

He made toast, then took his breakfast out to the deck, along with the morning edition of the *Globe*'s "Report on Business," which Rae had thoughtfully left folded to the TSE listings.

Share price was up again. Good news.

The wind was high that morning, rustling the pages as he tried to read his way through the paper. He was almost done when the phone rang.

Hoping it might be Rae, he dashed inside and answered on the third ring, only to hear his buddy on the line.

"How's the vacation going?" Harrison asked.

"Go to hell, Kincaid."

Harrison laughed. Then sobered up quickly. "I suppose I could have warned you. But I didn't want you to back out."

The tile floor was cold on his feet, so Aidan took the phone out to the sunny deck. "I didn't know she was pregnant."

"You're kidding."

"She didn't tell me. I guess she figured I'd hear via the grapevine."

"Everyone in the office assumed you knew. And they were all afraid to broach the subject."

"Yeah, well it was quite a shock to get out here and find Rae eight months pregnant."

"It must have been." Harrison waited a moment, then asked, "So how's it going?"

Aidan hesitated before answering, wondering if he should tell him. Then he decided, why not? He needed all the advice he could get. "Yesterday, I asked her to marry me."

"Attaboy! So when's the big day?"

If only. "She said no."

"What?" Harrison sounded stunned.

"Yeah. She wasn't exactly gracious about it, either."

"Look, buddy, Justine needs to drop by to pick up some clothes. How about we come over right now? We can talk about this some more."

"There's nothing more to talk about. But sure, drop by for those clothes."

HALF AN HOUR LATER, Harrison and Justine arrived at the summerhouse. They had Autumn with them, too. The little girl barely said hello before asking permission to play the piano.

"This is weird," Aidan said, closing the door. "Me welcoming you into your own home."

"I hope you've been making yourself comfortable?" Justine glowed in a turquoise sundress. Her strawberry blonde hair was pulled away from her face, exposing her lightly freckled neck and ears.

"Sure. It's been great. Thanks again for letting me use the place." As Autumn began to play, he raised his voice to be heard. "Should we go out to the deck?"

In the kitchen, he offered his visitors beer. Harrison said yes, but Justine stuck to water. Once outside, Justine asked, "Where's Rae?"

"She left a note saying she'd gone shopping, but that was two hours ago."

Justine wrinkled her nose as she slipped on a pair of sunglasses. "There aren't that many shops on the island."

"I know. I think she's avoiding me."

"Did she tell you why she didn't want to marry you?" Harrison opened the deck umbrella, then positioned a chair for Justine that would keep her in the shade.

Justine grinned at Aidan. "He insists on taking care of me. I'm growing to like it."

"Yeah, I'd say marriage suits you." He checked out Harrison, who was also looking pretty good these days. "Actually, it suits the pair of you."

"Now, what about Rae?" Justine asked. "Why is she so against the marriage idea?"

"She doesn't think a baby is a solid basis for a marriage. She isn't planning on keeping it, you know."

"Really?" Justine glanced at her husband, who shrugged his shoulders.

Before they could start judging Rae, Aidan rushed in to explain. "Rae isn't the maternal type, and she had some major issues with her own mother. She thinks the baby will be better off with adoptive parents. I have to admit, at first I thought she was right."

"And now?" Justine prodded.

"We were at the doctor's office yesterday. I couldn't help thinking that that was *my* kid inside her. Suddenly, Rae's logical solution to the problem seemed like the worst idea possible." Maybe he and Rae weren't perfect parent types like the Thompsons. But lots of parents had careers and babies, too. He supposed it took some juggling, but surely it wasn't impossible.

"Maybe she doesn't believe you're in this for the long haul," Justine speculated. "Perhaps she's thinking of the way you tossed her over when you banished her to Pittsburgh."

There was that word *banish* again. He was really starting to hate it. But he was also ready to admit that it was an accurate description of how he'd treated her. "I was scared and I panicked," he admitted. "Of course, if I'd known she was pregnant…"

"A woman wants to be loved for herself. Not because she's carrying a man's child. Though it's best of all when she has both."

Aidan caught the secret look passing between Justine and Harrison. So the rumors were true. "You're pregnant."

Harrison grinned. "It's official now. We told Nessa and Autumn this morning."

"Autumn's thrilled about being a big sister," Justine said.

"I'll bet she is. Congratulations." Aidan shook Harrison's hand and gave Justine a hug. He was glad for his friends, he really was, but he couldn't help contrasting their situation with his and Rae's.

Night and day, really.

From inside the house came the sound of someone opening the door. For a moment, Autumn stopped playing.

"Rae must be home." A sudden burst of adrenaline had him heading for the patio doors, but Justine stopped him.

"How about I talk to her first?" she suggested. "See how she's feeling?"

He supposed there was some logic to that idea, though he really wanted to see Rae now. Justine slipped off, leaving him alone with Harrison. Inside, the piano music started again.

"She's very talented," Aidan said.

Harrison nodded. "She takes after her mother. But I see a lot of Nessa and my mom in her, too."

"Do you?" Aidan hoped he didn't sound too eager. But he wanted nothing more than to believe that Autumn truly was Harrison's daughter in every sense of the word.

"I do."

Harrison looked at him intently and Aidan realized his friend was trying to tell him something.

"My relationship with Simone was an unusual one," Harrison said. "In many ways I was more like her big brother than her husband. I know it bothered her a lot that you didn't seem to like her."

Aidan said nothing.

"But things changed once your mother got sick, didn't they?"

Aidan closed his eyes. "Did she tell you what happened the night my mother died?"

"Simone was always honest with me. We had that much, at least." He clasped Aidan's shoulder. "I didn't blame you then. I still don't now."

Aidan couldn't believe his friend was

being this generous. "You're being very understanding. I'm not sure I deserve it."

"Are you kidding? You're my best friend. My right-hand man. You think I'd toss all that away because of one night?"

"I wish it hadn't happened. If I could change one thing from my past it would be that." Actually, he'd like to change two. Instead of transferring Rae, he should have asked her out again. Should have given their relationship a chance.

If he'd done that, she would have told him about the pregnancy and he would have had the opportunity to do the right thing, in the right way.

"Aidan, I'm a lucky man. My marriage to Simone might have been a challenge at times, but I'll always be grateful that I've been blessed with Autumn."

"Yes. She's something, all right." Aidan wanted to love the child, too, the way a proper godfather should. Maybe now that he and Harrison had cleared the air between them, he could start over with the little girl. The other night, when they'd made cookies together, it had seemed possible.

"Like I say, I've been lucky. I've got Autumn, and now I've got Justine, too."

"You both seem very happy."

"We're *partners,* Aidan. We like each other, we respect each other, and we have so much in common." He put a hand on Aidan's shoulder. "I think you and Rae could have that, as well."

CHAPTER SIXTEEN

"SO WHAT'S THIS ABOUT a missing little boy?" Justine asked.

The four of them—Harrison, Aidan, Rae and Justine—were having lunch outside on the deck under the shade of the canvas umbrella.

Rae had tried to retreat to her room, when she'd seen that they had guests. But Harrison had asked for her input on his plan to revamp the entire mergers and acquisitions department at Kincaid Communications and she hadn't been able to hold back her opinion.

Then he'd floored her by telling her that Aidan had recommended her to head the entire operation.

"He didn't?" Her gaze had flown to Aidan, but dark sunglasses shielded his eyes and his expression was completely enigmatic.

"I told you I'd spoken to Harrison about this," he said calmly.

Yes. But she hadn't really believed him at the time. She could hardly believe Harrison now.

"I'll have a written offer drawn up this week," Harrison said. "I hope you haven't become too attached to Pittsburgh."

Then Justine had come out of the house with a plate of sandwiches and a bowl of fruit salad. She'd obviously made full use of the groceries Rae had purchased in town.

Rae hadn't minded. She was starving. Yet, after only half a sandwich and a spoonful of the salad, she felt full. This baby was so big that Rae had next to no room left in her stomach.

Now she reclined in her chair and considered Justine's question about the missing boy.

"Didn't Nessa tell you? His name is Tyler Jenkins and he's only six years old."

"She mentioned something briefly, when Autumn was showing her father the tree house. But we didn't have time to go into the details." Justine leaned her elbows on the table. "I know the Jenkins family. I sold them their house three years ago, before Amanda got sick. What happened?"

"Tyler went missing the day I arrived on the island," Aidan explained. "Rae and I saw him on Pebble Beach that afternoon. I think we may have been the last people to see him before he disappeared. His father phoned the police the next morning, saying he hadn't come home for dinner as usual."

"Ted waited until the next morning to report this?" Justine sounded incredulous.

"He'd probably been too drunk to notice any sooner." Rae told them about her and Nessa's visit the next day. "The man was passed out at the kitchen table. He wasn't even trying to help find his son."

"I heard Ted started drinking when Amanda got sick," Justine said. "He couldn't deal with her prognosis. Everyone was hoping he'd pull himself together after her death."

"Well, he hasn't." Rae felt an uncomfortable pressure in her chest. Heartburn. Annie had given her tea to help with that. "Excuse me for a minute." She got up from the table to look for it.

Harrison followed her inside. "About that job, Rae. I hope you'll consider it? If you want to take some time off before you come back to work, that could be arranged."

She found the tin of dried leaves and dumped a spoonful of them into a mug. "I'm not taking any time off after the baby is born. I'm giving it up for adoption." She didn't look at Harrison as she said this. She had had enough of being judged for what was a thoughtful and perfectly reasonable decision.

"That's between you and Aidan. All I'm saying…"

"Aidan?" She couldn't let him get away with that. "This is my decision, Harrison. Mine alone."

"Isn't Aidan the father?"

"Of course, he is. But after the way he treated me—"

Harrison held out a hand to stop her. "I know transferring you from Seattle was harsh. But you have to understand something about Aidan. He doesn't give his affections easily. Ever since he was a kid, that's how he's been. When he does care, however, he cares with all his heart."

She'd been reaching for the tap. Now she froze and listened.

"As far as I know, Aidan has only loved four people in his life. He adored his mother, and he did everything humanly possible to help her when he learned that she was sick. He even accepted assistance from someone he despised—something that I know was very hard for him to do."

"You're talking about Simone."

"Yes." Harrison's gaze probed her face carefully. "He's told you about that I see. Good."

She didn't want to ask, but she couldn't stop herself. "Who are the other people Aidan loved?"

"Nessa and I were like his sister and brother. Our mothers were best friends and our families spent holidays together."

Yes, she'd seen the way he treated Nessa. And of course she knew of his close ties to Harrison. "And the fourth?"

Harrison leaned back against the counter, crossing his arms over his chest. His posture was laid-back, but his eyes on her were intense. "That would be you, Rae."

Rae couldn't breathe for a moment. In her head, she heard Harrison's last words repeated over and over and over. *That would be you, Rae.*

You, Rae.

You, Rae.

She put a steadying hand to the counter as her throat closed up and her eyes started to water. No. She couldn't cry. Not now. Not over this.

Puzzled lines creased Harrison's forehead. "I don't get it. Isn't that good news? Don't you love him, too?"

She wondered how such a smart man could be so blind.

"You're wrong," she finally choked out. "Aidan doesn't care about me. It's the baby he wants."

She recalled how tenderly Aidan had stroked her stomach yesterday. The way his eyes had gleamed when the doctor let him listen on the stethoscope to the fetal heart rate.

It was bloody ironic, really. After just a week and a half of knowing about it, Aidan had fallen in love with this baby. And she, the mother, still felt nothing. Nothing.

How could Aidan ever love a woman like that?

"I THINK RAE'S STILL bitter about the way you shuffled her off to Pittsburgh," Harrison told Aidan later.

Justine was up in the master bedroom, gathering the clothing she wanted to take back to Seattle. Rae was in her room, supposedly napping, though Aidan had his doubts. He'd seen the redness in her eyes when she'd excused herself.

Autumn was still playing the piano. The little girl was relentless. As she switched from a classical piece to one of Simone's jazz standards and began to sing, Aidan felt as if he was suffering from a heart attack. He stared, disbelieving, at Harrison, and his buddy gave him a rueful shrug.

"I know. Scary, isn't it?"

She was so much like her mother. It was like a visit from beyond the grave. "She's only seven," Aidan marveled.

"Just think how good she's going to be in

another ten years. Justine and I have talked a lot about it. My big concern is to make sure Autumn gets to be just a kid for as long as possible."

But Simone's adoring fans, devastated by their idol's premature death, would jump at the idea of Simone's daughter picking up where her mother had left off. A less scrupulous man than Harrison might have capitalized on this. But even if Harrison had wanted the money and craved the spotlight, he wasn't that sort of man.

"Autumn's lucky she has you to look out for her."

"And what about your child?" Harrison said bluntly. "Who's going to look out for him?"

Hell. Aidan had hoped they'd moved on from that topic. "I offered to marry Rae. And I stand by that offer. But it's Rae's choice and Rae doesn't want me—and she doesn't want the baby. I have to respect that."

"Don't talk to me about Rae's choices. The woman loves you, man. It's obvious. Just as you're clearly nuts about her."

"God, Harrison. Just because you're over

the moon about Justine doesn't mean you have to matchmake for all your single friends."

"I'm not doing this for all of them. Just the ones who're having a baby together."

"Would you butt out already? I haven't blasted you for setting us up in this house together, yet, but I really should."

"Come on, Aidan. We did you both a favor. Admit it."

"A favor would have been telling me she was pregnant. Not letting me walk in on her, eight months along, without a clue."

"I've already explained that. We thought you knew."

Yeah, everybody thought he knew. But that was history now. "Forget it, Harrison. Just forget it. The situation is way more complicated than you could ever understand."

"But—"

"No more matchmaking. I mean it. Now tell me what's been going on in Seattle while I've been gone."

ONCE HARRISON, JUSTINE and Autumn had left, Aidan went to run an errand, while Rae tried to relax with a recent bestseller. She was sitting right by the phone when it rang. She put down the book. "Hello?"

"May I please speak with Rae Cordell?"

"Speaking."

"Oh, good." The woman's voice brightened. "I'm Julia Thompson. Rae, I know you didn't want us to contact you—"

Suddenly short of breath, Rae undid the top button of her blouse. "That's right. I didn't. How did you get this number?"

Her brusque tone didn't deter the other woman.

"Your office gave it to me," she said, her tone still determinedly cheerful. "Your due date is so close now. My husband and I think of you all the time. I just had to tell you that. And we're so grateful—"

"You know I requested a closed adoption?" Rae got up from the armchair and headed for an open window. Oh, God, why had the idiots at her office passed on this phone number?

"Yes, but Rae—"

"Don't contact me again. The agency will let you know when—when you can have him."

"Him?" The other woman pounced on the pronoun.

"Or her."

"So you don't know—"

"No."

"Not that it matters to us, of course. We're so excited. We have the baby room all ready and I've been buying all these adorable—"

"Look. I'm glad you're excited. But don't call me again. Okay?" Rae pressed the end button, then hurled the phone across the room. It smashed on the wooden floor and the battery flew out.

"Rae?" Aidan stood in the foyer, a jug of milk in one hand.

For a moment they stared at each other. She drew a deep, shaky breath. "Damn phone companies. They never believe you when you say you're happy with your plan."

Aidan kept staring at her.

She couldn't take this. She just couldn't. "I need a change of scene. I think I'll go visit Annie."

She had to walk past him to get to the closet where she kept her purse and keys. He watched until she was about to walk out the door.

"Something tells me you shouldn't be driving right now."

She averted her gaze. "I'm fine. I just need…space."

She stepped past him and hurried to her car. As she headed down the road toward Lavender Farm, Rae tried not to replay the conversation with Julie Thompson in her head.

We're so happy, so grateful, so excited….

She turned on the radio. Jacked up the volume.

Don't think about it, Rae. Soon all this would be over, nothing more than a bad memory. She needed to focus on the future. It would be so much easier if she could accept the offer Harrison had promised to fax her. No doubt he would come up with a tempting package. The job itself was a once-in-a-lifetime opportunity.

But she had to turn it down. No way could she continue to work in proximity with Aidan when this was over. And though he'd offered to leave the company, she couldn't expect him to do that. Especially not after

Harrison had made it so clear just how tight the ties between the two families were.

No, she needed to move on, but to what and to where…. She had no idea. Somehow the future seemed unfathomable right now.

Spotting something on the road ahead, Rae took her foot off the gas pedal. The cows were out of their pasture again. What had Aidan called them? Kerries, that was it.

Rae reduced her speed to a crawl and was forced to come to a complete halt when one of the cows stopped on her side of the road and gave her a baleful glare.

"What?" she asked the animal. "I'm just trying to get to my friend's house. Is that so wrong?"

Then she noticed the calf. The sturdy little thing came up from the other side of the road and crossed over to what was obviously its mother. The cow stopped glaring, nudged her calf toward the rest of the herd, then followed.

As she started moving again, Rae noticed that three vehicles had been stopped behind her. Someone should call the local radio station and report the traffic jam. She smiled at her little joke, then checked the rearview mirror.

Wait a minute. What was that car behind the truck? She waited until a rise in the road gave her the angle she needed to see more clearly.

Sure enough, Aidan's sporty convertible was two vehicles behind her.

Good God, couldn't he let her out of his sight for a few hours? What was he so worried about, anyway? No matter where she went on the island, she'd never be more than an hour's drive from the clinic. Plus, she had Annie lined up to be her labor coach.

Everything was organized. Nothing to worry about.

Except for the fact that she suddenly felt as if she needed to vomit.

Rae opened the side window and sucked in a breath of ocean-scented air. She wasn't going to be sick. She wasn't going to be sick…. She wasn't—

Ah. Her stomach heaved. Not enough to spill its contents, but this was a definite warning. She signaled to the right, then pulled over to the edge of the road.

She waited until the truck behind her passed by, then scurried out of her seat and headed for the shallow ditch. She didn't see Aidan's car, or the vehicle that had been behind his. She was too busy retching into the tall grass that bordered the road.

She'd hated throwing up ever since she was a kid. She'd fight the nauseous feeling as long as she could, even though she knew she'd feel better if she just allowed her body to do what it needed to do.

Her stomach heaved for the third time, even though there was nothing more left. Rae sputtered, wishing she'd thought to bring paper towels or a bottle of water in the car with her.

"Here," Aidan said.

A towel fluttered before her and she grabbed at it. Aidan. Great. He was seeing her at her best, yet again.

CHAPTER SEVENTEEN

RAE WIPED OFF HER FACE, then tried to clean her tongue of the horrible taste of bile.

"Water?" Aidan passed her an open bottle.

Of course, he'd have everything she needed. "Thanks," she said thickly. She filled her mouth, swirled the water around, then spit it out.

Was there any level on which pregnancy didn't suck?

"Feeling okay?"

"Never better," she lied. She glanced at him, and then looked away. Damn, it really wasn't fair that she was so...big, with the smell of vomit all around her, while he looked like someone who should be standing at the helm of a yacht.

"So," he said, his tone as calm as if he'd

just watched her tie her shoelaces. "On your way to Lavender Farm?"

"That was the plan." She needed to see Annie. For some reason she found the woman's company comforting, even though they had absolutely nothing in common.

"How about I drive you the rest of the way? In case you get sick again. We'll take your car, since it's easier for you to get in and out of."

"What about your convertible?"

"We'll pick it up on the way back."

She didn't want to agree to his plan, but it seemed plain bullheaded to argue since her stomach was definitely still queasy.

He held out his hand, and again—because it would have seemed rude to do otherwise—she took it.

"So did Harrison try to strong-arm you into accepting the promotion?" he asked, once they were settled and driving again.

"He made the offer pretty tempting. But don't worry. I'm planning to refuse."

"Why?"

"You know why. We can't work together after this." She plucked a blade of grass from her shirt and released it through the open window.

"Rae. Please. I don't want to do you out of your career. If you don't want to work together, then *I'll* go to Pittsburgh." He smiled.

She didn't smile back.

She hated it when he was nice to her. When he was nice, she liked him. And when she liked him, she began to think that the man she'd fallen in love with in Seattle might have been the real Aidan, after all.

And that made her want to accept his proposal. Which was something she couldn't do, because as much as Aidan seemed to be in denial, she knew the truth. She couldn't be a mother. It always came back to that, didn't it?

Rae closed her eyes and pretended to sleep. It seemed her only safe refuge for the moment.

NESSA PULLED HER CAR into the Jenkins's driveway. Her foot felt heavy as she lifted it off the brake. If her symptoms got any worse, she might have to stop driving. The thought was sobering. She knew she couldn't live independently on the island without a car.

"That's not going to happen," she promised herself, as she parked in the empty spot by the side of the house. The truck that had been here the previous time she'd visited was gone. She grabbed her walking stick, then struggled out of the car and made her way to the front door.

No one responded when she knocked.

With some effort, she went round the house, peering in windows, looking for signs of occupation. Perhaps Ted was passed out somewhere?

But then where was his truck?

Was it possible he'd found work? Or was he actually out looking for his son? Now that was a happy thought.

On impulse, she checked his mailbox and found a few fliers and a hydro bill. Frustrated, she returned to the front door and tried the handle. It was locked.

"He's gone."

She whirled around at the sound of a female voice. A woman holding two golden retrievers on leashes was standing on the road.

"Excuse me? I'm looking for Ted Jenkins."

"So were the police about an hour ago. But he left early this morning. Probably caught the first ferry. I saw him when I let the dogs out for their morning constitutional. He was hauling two heavy-looking suitcases."

Nessa knew a lot of the people who lived on Summer Island, but she'd never met this woman before. She was in her sixties, with skin that had weathered decades of sun and wind.

"I'm Nessa Kincaid. Tyler used to come to my day care."

"Ah. Gabe Brooke's wife." The woman absently scratched one of her dogs under his collar.

"Ex-wife." It figured that this woman would know Gabe. Besides owning the local newspaper and real estate business, he also sat on the Island Trust, the governing equivalent of a city mayor.

"I'm Ellie Rubin. I live next door." She pointed to the cottage on the south side of the road. It was far better maintained than the Jenkinses'.

"Nice to meet you, Ellie. Do you have

any idea where Ted Jenkins was heading this morning?"

"No. But I'm guessing we won't be seeing him again soon. He was being pretty quiet and sneaky. I guess he didn't want anyone knowing he was skipping out without his boy."

But *had* he been leaving without Tyler? Nessa tried not to think about those heavy suitcases. No. That was too Stephen King for Summer Island.

"You say the police were by earlier?"

"Yeah. Dex Ulrich. You know him?"

She nodded and hoped her cheeks didn't turn too pink. "So Dex knows Ted Jenkins skipped town?"

"He does."

"Okay." Nessa let out a discouraged sigh. She'd woken this morning determined to do something proactive about finding Tyler. With Autumn gone, she had lots of time. She'd thought that talking to his father again would be a good place to start.

Now she didn't know what to do.

"Did you see Tyler the day he disappeared?" she asked Ellie.

"Saw him in the morning, on his way out

the door. Tyler didn't hang around much when his father was drinking."

"I guess he wouldn't."

"He wasn't a stupid boy," Ellie agreed.

Nessa noticed her use of the past tense. "Do you think he's still alive, Ellie?"

"Honestly? No, I don't, but I can't tell you why. It's just a feeling I have." She glanced at the Jenkins house again, then away. "Well, I'd better get these guys home and feed them."

The dogs immediately stood at attention, as if they'd understood her.

"Thanks, Ellie. It was nice to meet you." Using her cane, Nessa made her way back to her car.

The older woman watched her for a while, then led her dogs back to her house. They'd disappeared inside by the time Nessa backed her car onto the road.

INSTEAD OF HEADING for home, Nessa stopped at Derby's in town for a coffee. She ordered a slice of blackberry pie, as well, and the young female server had just brought it to her, when another patron entered the diner.

Nessa worked to keep her features impassive as her ex-husband made his grand entrance. Every female in the room, whether eighteen or eighty, turned to look.

To be honest, it wasn't his fault. Gabe didn't try to stand out in a crowd. Genetics and a flawless set of chromosomes were one hundred percent to blame.

Maybe he won't notice me. Nessa sipped her coffee, holding the cup as a partial shield. Maybe she wouldn't eat this pie, after all. She'd just leave some money on the table and slip out when—

"Nessa. Would you mind if I joined you?"

Gabe's tone was nothing if not polite and civil. Those adjectives pretty much summed up their entire relationship: courtship, marriage, even their divorce. All of it had passed by without so much as a ripple of passion. At least not on Gabe's side.

Realizing she'd taken too long to answer, Nessa said quickly, "Of course not. Sit down."

He slid into the bench seat across from her and she was glad he couldn't see the cane tucked under her seat. Now she'd have to wait for him to leave first, so he wouldn't see how pronounced her limp had become.

"I've been thinking about you lately," he said, after the server took his order for coffee.

Of course he hadn't ordered pie. Gabe never indulged in sweets. He was too conscious of his physique.

Again, Nessa was aware that she wasn't really being fair. Gabe didn't have a sweet tooth. And he didn't need to watch his weight, either. Playing tennis almost every day kept him in excellent shape.

"Tyler Jenkins goes to your day care, doesn't he?"

"He did last year," she agreed.

"I'm sorry, Nessa. I know you must be worried about him."

She blinked, surprised at the compassion in his voice. The Gabe she'd married had never seemed to care about how she felt. But then Gabe had changed since he'd found out about her MS. The diagnosis had been one big wake-up call for both of them.

Too bad he'd hurt her so many times by then that she'd had no room in her heart to give him a second chance.

"I just drove by his place, Gabe. His

neighbor told me that Ted has left the island. She said he took a lot of stuff with him."

"That doesn't sound promising."

"No. Do you know Ted? Do you think he could have killed his own son?"

"For a while he was on the *Courier* payroll. He was the deliveryman for the north end of the island. We had to let him go when we found out he was drinking and driving...." He shook his head, disparagingly. "The man had a temper on him, too. Coupled with his drinking, I'd have to say it's possible he did something to Tyler. What does Dex think?"

Nessa stared down at her pie. "How would I know?"

Gabe took a sip of his coffee. "I heard you've been seeing quite a bit of him lately."

She felt her cheeks heat up and told herself not to be foolish. She was a free woman now. She didn't need to feel guilty about seeing another man. "Dex and I have been friends for a long time. You know that."

"But now you're more than friends?"

She hesitated. "We're very good friends. That's it."

His chest rose as he inhaled and she saw real sorrow in his eyes when he forced a smile. "I'm not sure I believe that."

She shrugged. "I guess you can believe what you want."

"Well, he's a good man, at least. And you deserve the best for a change, Nessa."

Since she'd been fourteen years old, she'd thought Gabe was the best. Even now, with so much painful history between them, she could remember how he had once set her heart blazing with just a look in her direction, a smile.

Despite her best intentions, she felt herself softening. Gabe had made her so unhappy, but she didn't want to see him suffer unnecessarily. "What about you, Gabe? Are you seeing anyone?"

He made a slight face, as if his coffee had turned bitter. "It's still too soon for me. I can't forgive myself for what I did to you. What I lost. It's a big house for one person, you know?"

"Oh, Gabe." For a moment she wished that she could give him another chance. But the old hurt was still there. She could feel it, pushing her away from him, even while a part of her longed to give him comfort.

He took another swallow of his coffee, then set a twenty on the table. Too much money, but that was Gabe's way.

"Take care of yourself, Nessa. It was good to see you." He touched her hand briefly, then stood and made his way out of the diner. The females in the room noted his exit, too, much as they'd witnessed his arrival fifteen minutes earlier.

The door opened just as Gabe was reaching for it and Dex entered the café, forcing Gabe to step back to make room. Gabe's back straightened as he sized up the other man in one quick glance. Dex reacted with a similar, wary assessment. If the men had been peacocks, Nessa mused, their feathers would have been on full display.

A few words were exchanged, but Nessa was too far away to hear what they were. Gabe continued on his way out the door while Dex looked around the café. When his glance lit on her, he gave a brief smile then set out toward her.

"May I join you?"

"Of course. Please sit down." Why would he think he had to ask?

Dex picked up the menu from the stainless steel holder at the side of the table and tapped the edge against the table.

"You've heard Ted Jenkins left the island?" she asked.

"Yes. We've put a bulletin out on him, but haven't heard anything so far. He didn't take the ferry…. He may have caught a ride on a fishing boat. How did you know he was gone?"

"I went by his house this morning and spoke to Ellie Rubin. She was out walking her dogs."

The server came and Dex placed an order for coffee and pie. Then, still holding the menu between them, Dex asked, "So, how's Gabe?"

"Okay, I guess."

Dex fixed his gaze on the menu. "He still loves you."

"We're divorced, Dex."

"Doesn't matter. He's still hung up on you. I can tell."

"Well, maybe he is. But it's too little, too late. You know what he was like when we were married. He didn't love me then, when he had the chance."

"Bloody fool."

She smiled. "Thanks, Dex."

The server came with his pie and coffee. She refilled Nessa's cup, too, and left.

"I was wondering if I could take you to dinner tonight, Nessa. I made reservations at the Owl's Nest."

"I'd love to have dinner with you, but we don't have to go there. Let's just grab something at the Cliffside."

"But I want to take you somewhere…special."

Dex looked at her, his expression guarded, yet hopeful. It was impossible not to understand his intention. He wanted to romance her. To take their relationship to the next level.

Nessa moved her foot, until it was resting on the cane she'd placed under the seat. Whenever she talked about her MS with her brother and her friends, she always reminded them that the majority of MS victims didn't end up in a wheelchair. Many were lucky enough to live normal, or close-to-normal lives. She spoke this way, assuming that she would be one of the fortunate ones.

But in just one week her condition had deteriorated so markedly that she had to consider the other possibility. That she would end up in a chair. Possibly in an institution.

How could she blithely enter into a relationship with Dex, knowing that she could be sentencing him to life with a severely disabled woman?

"Dex, I've been meaning to talk to you about what happened between us the other afternoon."

She saw the alarm in his eyes. *Don't be hurt, Dex. Please understand I'm doing this for you.*

"That afternoon was wonderful. One of the best of my life. But I don't think we should be moving in that direction right now."

Dex stared back at her, his expression suddenly distant. He didn't believe her. He thought this was just a line.

It pained her to see how she'd wounded him. She wished she could recant and tell him the truth. That she'd love to go to the Owl's Nest with him. To make love with him later tonight, and many times over in the years to come.

But how many years would they have? What if it turned out to be only months?

"I value our friendship so much, Dex. I'm afraid to risk losing it."

He pulled out a twenty-dollar bill and set it on the table.

Just like Gabe. It would have been funny, if it hadn't been so terribly sad.

"Please, Dex. I want us to still be friends." She couldn't accept his love, but did she have to give up everything?

"Of course," he said. "If you ever need anything, just give me a call."

He left and she knew that it was over, all of it. The friendly meals at the Cliffside, the walks along the beach, the phone conversations that came when she seemed to need them the most. He thought she was rejecting him, and so he'd rejected her, too.

Nessa waited until she was sure Dex would be long gone, then she reached under the seat for her cane. There was forty dollars on the table now. Probably one of the best tips the server would ever get.

But Nessa would never order blackberry pie here again.

CHAPTER EIGHTEEN

WHEN RAE AND AIDAN arrived at the bed-and-breakfast, Jennifer was mixing ingredients in the largest bowl Rae had ever seen. They'd entered via the kitchen door, and now they were sitting at the counter, watching Jennifer work.

"Justine's three months along," Jennifer said. "That means she'll be having her baby in January or February. I wonder if she'll quit work or just take time off?"

Aidan speculated on the answer, but Rae didn't pay much attention. She'd never been in a farmhouse kitchen before, and though this was technically a bed-and-breakfast, Jennifer's kitchen was exactly what she'd imagined one to be like. The cupboards were pine and the color accents were blue and yellow. Copper pans hung from a rack over one counter. A big ceramic jug full of cooking utensils stood next to the stove.

As she spoke, Jennifer scooped flour from a large tub into the bowl. *Without measuring,* Rae marveled. A moment later, Jennifer pulled a large jug of iced tea out of the fridge and offered some to her guests.

Jennifer was one of those quiet people who managed to accomplish a lot while no one was noticing. Even her beauty was the understated sort. Her blond hair was quite striking, when it wasn't tied back.

She doesn't try to be anything but herself, Rae thought, watching Jennifer dump raisins, dried cranberries and white chocolate chunks into the mixture.

Aidan's friend puzzled Rae, because while Jennifer seemed to be living a life she loved and doing things she was talented at, she didn't seem overly happy.

In fact, at times she looked downright sad.

Aidan reached over to dip his finger into the batter. Jennifer didn't seem to mind. "Taste good?" she asked.

"Sure it does. What are you making?"

"Fruit and nut scones for tomorrow's breakfast. We have a full house, as usual."

Maybe that was good news from a financial perspective, but Rae thought Jennifer looked tired. "Summer is obviously your busy season," she said. "Do you get to relax in the winter?"

"I used to." Jennifer's gaze traveled to a bulletin board on the side of the fridge. "Simone and I had some fabulous trips together."

Rae went to examine the postcards and snapshots. There were lots of the two girl-friends in Europe and New York City.

"Don't any of your other friends like to travel?" she asked Jennifer. Simone had been dead for two years. And if the mementos on this board were anything to go on, Jennifer hadn't taken a trip since.

"They do, but Simone had a way of making things happen. She'd arrange for someone to stay here to take care of the work and to cook for my father. Of course, now I have the baby and my aunt to worry about, too. Though my brother and sister-in-law will be picking up Erica next week."

"Annie seems pretty self-reliant," Rae said.

"She is in most ways. The problem with my aunt is that she takes on too much. She goes hiking in the forest and is gone for hours. Then she squirrels away in her cottage, concocting all these teas and potions. Lately, she's been especially busy on some project or other—I think it has something to do with your labor. She won't let me near the cottage to clean. The other day she wouldn't even allow me in to strip the bed."

"She didn't want me coming inside, either," Rae said. "I didn't know she was working on something special."

"I wonder what her project is?" Aidan went to the window and gazed across the yard.

Curious, Rae joined him. Annie's cottage sat beyond the flower gardens, tucked next to a magnificent arbutus tree. Characteristic strips of cinnamon-colored bark had peeled from the smooth, twisted branches. As she admired the beauty of the unusual evergreen, she noticed something stir amid the deep green leaves.

"Did you see that?" Aidan asked.

She nodded. "Do you think it was a squirrel?"

"It seemed bigger to me. Closer to a monkey size."

Jennifer laughed. "We don't have monkeys on the island, Aidan."

His face tensed and his eyes widened. "No. But you have the next best thing. You have little boys. Excuse me a minute." Aidan exited through the back door and started to run.

CHAPTER NINETEEN

"WHERE'S HE GOING?" Jennifer asked. Her hands were deep inside the large ceramic bowl, kneading the fruit-and-nut-studded dough.

Rae didn't take the time to answer. She was right behind Aidan, pulling open the screen door, scrambling down the steps, trying her best to run.

Aidan was so far ahead of her he'd almost reached the tree. She wanted to move faster, but all of a sudden her body told her, no. Stop.

She felt as if a fat elastic band had tightened around her midsection. The pressure started so quickly, she had to gasp for breath. She placed both hands on her belly and felt the power of the contraction.

Even though she'd never had one before, she knew that was what this was.

Holy cow, she was going into labor.

A few seconds passed. Aidan was at the tree, calling up into the branches and holding out his hands, but she was focused on herself now, on her body. She felt the tension slowly ease. The pain vanished, as if it had never been there.

Okay. She had survived the first contraction and it hadn't been so bad after all. No need to stress or push the panic button. This could be a false alarm. And even if it wasn't, first-timers were in labor for hours and hours. Sometimes days.

She straightened and resumed walking toward the tree. Jennifer came out of the house and easily caught up to her.

"Have you figured out what's going on yet?" Her hands still had bits of dough clinging to them, which she picked at absently as she walked.

"I'm not positive," Rae admitted. "But I think Aidan has found Tyler Jenkins."

Aidan had decided to climb the tree rather than stay on the ground yelling. She watched him swing up onto the lowest branch, then stand, keeping a stabilizing hand on the trunk.

Jennifer watched him skeptically. "Tyler lives on the south end of the island. That's thirty miles from here."

"I'm only guessing, but your Aunt Annie probably had something to do with this." Rae glanced back at the cottage. Sure enough, Annie's face was pressed against one of the windowpanes. A second later, the face disappeared.

"Come on, Tyler," Aidan said. "Let me help you down."

A few seconds passed. The upper branches rustled again.

"If you're trying to hide, Tyler, it isn't working. I can see you from here."

Could he? Rae went closer and looked up. She spotted a boy's running shoe. A leg clad in denim. What would a six-year-old boy in Tyler's situation be thinking right now?

Probably he'd be scared.

"It's okay, Tyler," she said. "No one's going to be angry at you."

A few seconds passed. Then she heard a sniff.

"My dad'll be mad."

Aidan grinned down at her and gave her a

thumbs-up. Rae's heart lifted at this confirmation that they'd found the missing boy.

"Your dad has left the island," Aidan said. "I'm not sure where he's gone, but he probably won't be back for a while."

"Really? Is that the truth?" The hopeful note in the boy's voice spoke volumes for the way he really felt about his father.

"It is," Rae confirmed. "Come down from the tree, Tyler. Everything's going to be okay."

The branches rustled again. A second foot settled on the limb next to the first one.

"I—I'm not so sure I can get down."

"I'll help, bud." Aidan reached up until he had a grip on one of Tyler's legs. "Step down. I'll make sure you don't fall."

With Aidan's guidance, Tyler was soon on the main branch, and then he jumped the rest of the distance into Jennifer's arms.

"Everyone is going to be so glad that you're okay." Jennifer hugged him close before setting him on the ground.

Rae hugged him, too, elated that they'd found him and he really was all right. But as she took a closer look at him, she saw a faint discoloration on one side of his face.

Old bruises? "You are okay, aren't you?" She frowned and glanced over at Aidan. From the look he gave her, she realized he'd reached the same conclusion about the colored marks.

"I'm fine," Tyler said quickly. "I was just staying with Aunt Annie. It was a secret," he added quietly. "I was s'posed to stay in the cabin, but I got bored."

Finally, the cottage door opened and Annie emerged. Tyler went running for her and she crouched low so they could talk face-to-face.

"Are you mad at me?" he asked. "I wrecked the secret."

Annie looked Jennifer straight in the eyes. Then Aidan. Then Rae. "No, I'm not mad," she told the little boy, her tone slightly defiant. "It was time for our secret to end, I think."

Tyler looked relieved. "Yeah. I was getting tired of having to stay inside all the time."

"It's been a long time," Aidan said. "Did you know there were helicopters looking for you? And search parties and the Coast Guard?" As he spoke he looked directly at Annie.

"Helicopters?" Tyler said. "Cool! I wished I coulda seen them."

"I'm sorry," Annie said quietly. "I know a lot of people were worried, but I'll bet Tyler's father wasn't one of them."

"Speaking of people worrying, I'd better phone the police," Jennifer said. "Tyler, would you like to come to the house with me and have a snack? I made cookies earlier this morning."

His eyes grew wide. "I know. I could smell them."

Jennifer laughed and held out her hand. Without a backward glance at Annie or any of them, Tyler went with her.

When he was out of hearing range, Aidan said, "Annie? I hope you've got a good story for the cops when they get here."

"I'll just tell them the truth. It started three weeks ago, when I was in for an appointment with Dr. Marshall. Tyler's father was in the waiting room, too. I guess he'd brought Tyler in because of some stomach problem, but I heard the doctor mutter when they were gone. She said something like, 'that man doesn't deserve to be a father.'"

"So Dr. Marshall knew something wasn't right."

Annie nodded. "A few days later I was picking up eggs for Jennifer at the Red Door Farm."

"Isn't that close to Tyler's house?"

"Yes, it's about a quarter mile up the road. Anyway, I was driving by, real slow with all my windows open because it was a nice night, when I heard a child crying.... Actually, screaming," she modified. "I slowed down even more and that's when Tyler came running out of his house. I could see right away that he'd been hurt."

"Do you remember what day that was?" Rae asked.

"Sure." Annie gave her the date.

"So Ted lied," Rae said. "Tyler did come home for dinner that night."

"And his no-good father beat him badly." Annie's voice quivered, despite the firm set to her mouth. "Tyler told me it was because he'd gotten his shorts dirty."

Rae looked at Aidan, who shook his head, his expression dark. "The bastard," he muttered.

"I told Tyler to get in my truck. That I'd help him." Annie's eyes, a little glazed with age but still sharp with wisdom, fixed on Aidan first, then Rae. "I took him home and I told him that he was going to stay with me for a while. I made a herb poultice for his bruises. Luckily, no bones were broken, because he had bruises all over his back, too."

"That monster!" Rae wished she'd done some damage to Ted Jenkins when she'd had the chance.

"You never thought to call the police?" Aidan asked.

Annie spit on the ground. "So they could send another social worker out and suggest a new and improved anger management course for the father? I know the way the system works. They always try to keep the family together. Well, that's okay in most circumstances, but not for Tyler. I simply couldn't let that child go back there."

"So you wrote a letter to Ted Jenkins?" It made sense now, Rae thought. Really, it made perfect sense.

"Sure, I did." Annie smiled proudly. "And my plan worked, didn't it? Ted Jenkins left. That's proof enough of his guilt."

"You're right about that," Aidan said. "But I wonder what will happen to Tyler now?"

"He'll go to a good home," Annie predicted. "I won't stand for anything else."

As she spoke, a police cruiser turned down the lane. Rae recognized Dex Ulrich at the wheel. He waved and stopped the car.

"Tyler's in the house," Aidan called out to him.

Dex nodded, then drove farther, before parking and rushing inside.

"Well, time to face the music, I guess," Annie muttered. She squared her shoulders and headed for the house, as well.

Rae was about to follow when another contraction started. Her hands flew to her belly as she stopped and caught her breath.

"You okay?" Aidan asked.

She didn't want to tell him what was happening. It was too soon. And she still hoped this would turn out to be false labor. After all, a full fifteen minutes had passed since that first contraction.

"I'm fine." She took a deep breath, then another, waiting for the pain to crescendo, then fade.

Aidan frowned, but he didn't question her any further. Once she could walk again, he took her by the arm and led her toward the farmhouse.

"They won't put Annie in jail, will they?" Rae asked.

"Knowing Dex, I highly doubt it. He'll make sure no criminal charges are filed. I can't see Ted Jenkins laying any civil charges in this case, either."

Aidan slid his arm around her shoulders and held her tightly. "Are you sure you're okay? You were looking quite pale for a moment there."

"Just a little indigestion."

"Hmm," Aidan said. Then he opened the back door and they were in Jennifer's kitchen again. Tyler was at the table, in front of a plate of cookies and a half-empty glass of milk. Dex sat across from him, hands folded on the table. He was asking questions, and, in between bites, Tyler was answering them.

Closer to the door, by the sink, Jennifer had her hands on her hips and was speaking to her aunt in a quiet, but exasperated voice.

Giving her a lecture, no doubt. As soon as Jenn saw them, though, she paused.

"I'm sorry," Jenn said. "I had no idea my aunt was hiding Tyler in her cottage." She glanced worriedly at Dex, who was still focused on the boy. "He hasn't told me what's going to happen now."

"Don't worry." Aidan gave his friend a quick hug. "I'm sure everything will work out. The main thing is that Tyler is safe, right?"

Jenn nodded.

"Well, don't expect me to apologize," Annie said stubbornly. "That boy needed help and I had to do something."

"Fine. You had to do something. But Auntie, taking a six-year-old child from his home is *kidnapping*. Don't you understand that?"

Annie bristled defensively, but Rae didn't hear her response. A third contraction was starting. She hung back near the door and hoped no one would notice her.

This was too soon. Just five minutes since the last one. And powerful, as well. Much stronger than the first two.

She closed her eyes and tried to breathe through the pain and stay calm. Why was this happening now? She had two more weeks before her due date, damn it.

"Rae?"

No mistaking the worry in Aidan's voice now. She tried to answer him, but couldn't catch her breath. He turned to Annie, as if seeking advice.

The midwife looked at him as if he was an idiot. "Don't just stand there, Aidan. Take her to the clinic. Can't you see your woman's in labor?"

OF COURSE SHE WAS. Aidan had guessed that was what was happening, but he'd been a little frightened to admit it. It seemed as if he'd only just found out Rae was pregnant. Now she was about to have the baby.

His baby.

Their baby.

He went to Rae and held on to her gently but protectively. She was breathing the way Annie had taught her to. Listening to the pattern of her breaths, and watching the way she held her belly, he could tell when the contraction ended.

"Think you can make it to the car?" he asked.

"Of course, I can make it to the car. I had a contraction, I didn't break my leg. But there isn't any hurry. I've only just started. We've got hours to go."

"Don't be so sure," Annie contradicted her. "I have a feeling you're going to progress pretty quickly." She turned to Aidan. "Rae refuses to believe me, but her body was made for having babies."

Aidan nodded, getting the message loud and clear. Get to the clinic. Get to the clinic, now. He took Rae's arm and attempted to lead her outside.

She shook him off and went to Annie. "You have to come, too. You're my labor coach."

Annie patted her hand. "You're going to be fine, Rae. You don't need me."

"But I can't do this alone!" Rae gasped and clutched her belly again.

Another contraction. Even stronger than the previous ones, if Rae's tortured expression was any indicator.

"Rae, will you please come?" he implored. "Or are you going to have our baby on the kitchen floor?"

Finally, Dex looked over at them. "You'd better listen to Aidan and let him drive you to the clinic, Rae. Annie can't help you now. I'm taking her in to the station. She's got a lot of explaining to do."

THE DAY SHE'D BEEN dreading was finally here. Rae leaned back into the car seat and breathed in, breathed out, with the next contraction.

They were just terrible now. And only three or four minutes apart. Why was everything happening so quickly?

Between breaths, she cried, "I can't do this!" She moaned as the pain tightened. Gasped as it grew stronger. "I can't, Aidan. I just can't."

He was driving and fumbling with his wallet at the same time. "I've got the doctor's emergency number here somewhere."

She'd tell him to pull over for safety reasons, but right now dying in a head-on crash sounded like a good idea. Or…they could sail over a cliff like Thelma and Louise. That would be pretty cool, too.

"Here it is." He closed his fingers round the business card he'd taken at the last appointment. "Are you between contractions now?"

"Yes." And already dreading the onslaught of the next one. She eyed the time display on the dash and cringed as another minute passed by.

"Dial the number on my cell, would you? The guy behind me probably thinks I'm drunk by the way I've been weaving all over the road."

She glanced out the rear window and saw a farmer in a pickup, shaking his head at them. A moment later, they passed Aidan's convertible where he'd left it on the side of the road.

"Okay." She punched in the numbers and pressed Send. On the dashboard, another minute ticked by.

With inevitable stealth, she felt the muscles in her abdomen begin to tighten. "Oh, hell. Here we go again." She tossed Aidan the phone just as someone came on the line.

Deep breath in, Rae. Relax. Float above the pain. She did her best to conjure Annie's voice, but bits and pieces of Aidan's conversation broke through her concentration.

"About three minutes apart," she heard him say. Then, "We're on our way. About ten minutes."

Would they make it? She didn't want this to end in her stupid rental car. Could anything be worse than that?

"Hurry, Aidan. Damn it, can't this thing go any faster?"

"Faster? Rae, we're in a Ford. Not a Lamborghini."

She flopped back in her seat as the contraction ended. "They're getting stronger," she said. "I'm surprised my—"

She felt a gush of warm water between her legs. Oh, why hadn't she kept her mouth shut?

"What happened?" Aidan glanced at her seat, and at the liquid soaking her shorts and pooling on the floor.

"My water broke. Don't you know anything?" If only she could do this birth thing by proxy. And now her midwife wasn't even going to be there. "Can't you call a lawyer and get Annie released? I need all the help I can get."

Aidan lifted his foot from the accelerator as they entered the town limits. She cursed.

"Why are you slowing down?"

"Do you want me to hit a pedestrian? Calm down, Rae. We're almost there."

Calm down? That was easy for him to say.

He pulled into the clinic parking lot, near the back of the building. A nurse waited at the open side door. She smiled and waved as she spotted them. Instead of feeling relief, Rae was paralyzed by the sudden onset of terror.

They were at the clinic. There were doctors and nurses here. This was going to happen. It was so, so real.

Aidan threw the gearshift into park and turned to face her. He took her hands, squeezed them gently.

"Look at me, Rae. You can do this."

She felt tears spilling from her eyes. Her teeth chattered. "N-no. I can't. C-can't do it alone."

"You're not alone. I know I'm not Annie, but I'll come with you. We'll ask about the pain. Hopefully, they'll have something to help you."

But in that instant, Rae suddenly understood where her fear was coming from. All the craziness of the past nine months, the wild mood swings, the crying, the insomnia.

The moment she'd been dreading was before her....

And it wasn't the labor she was so afraid of. It was giving up her baby.

CHAPTER TWENTY

SHE *HAD* TO GIVE UP the baby. Rae knew this. She wasn't mother material. It would be cruel to keep this child and subject it to a miserable childhood.

She'd kept her resolve this far. Now she just had to get through the next twenty-four hours.

Aidan helped her out of the car and into the building. The nurse—her name was Irene, Rae recalled—gave her a towel to dry off with, then helped her into the birthing room. Within minutes of arrival, Rae was prone and in another of those abysmal hospital gowns.

Be strong, she told herself again, as the nurse performed a quick internal examination between the contractions.

"You're eight centimeters, already," she said in disbelief. "This is going to happen really soon." She glanced at her watch. "I hope the doctor makes it."

Rae rolled her eyes at Aidan. *Um, yeah. Me, too.*

He smiled, showing that he understood what she was thinking. He closed his hand over hers and squeezed.

Thank God he was here with her. He didn't have Annie's experience and know-how, but she needed him all the same.

A contraction rolled in. They were like waves, Rae decided. Waves of pain that were trying to suck her under. But she wouldn't let them. Now that she understood the nature of her fear, she was determined to rise above it.

"It's too late to offer you an epidural," the nurse said. "But we have other options for pain relief. Would you like me to explain them to you?"

She shook her head, no. She could handle this. It would be better for the baby without drugs.

"Rae, are you sure?" Aidan looked over at the nurse. "What do you have that would make this easier for her?"

"No drugs," Rae insisted. A good, healthy

start. That was the last gift she would give to this baby.

"One more question, Rae." The nurse came to her side and took her other hand. "I know you're planning to give the child up for adoption. But do you want to hold your baby for a few minutes after the birth?"

For some reason Rae thought of Tyler jumping down from the tree and remembered the moment she'd wrapped her arms around the little boy. The joy of knowing he was alive, he was safe, he was well.

She'd never hugged a child before. And she'd never held a baby.

"No." She forced her mind to go blank. There was only room for one thought. *Be strong.* She had to be strong. "I most definitely do not want to hold the baby."

AT THE RCMP DETACHMENT, Nessa was admitted to the bull pen area where Dex and several of his constables were gathered in quiet conversation. Everyone fell silent at the sight of her.

"Thank you for calling, Dex. I can't believe it's finally over. Tyler's all right!"

She'd gone straight to her car after Dexter's

phone call. He'd been brief, his tone curt and businesslike as he informed her that Tyler Jenkins had been found at Annie's cottage on Lavender Farm.

"Can I see him?" she'd asked.

"Since he knows you well, that's probably a good idea," he'd replied, but there'd been no welcome in his voice.

She took a few steps forward, trying to minimize her use of the cane. She was aware of the surreptitious surveillance of everyone in the room. She winced as Dex's hard expression softened with pity.

She lifted her chin. She couldn't see Tyler anywhere. "Where is he?"

Dex cleared his throat, then met her gaze directly, but only briefly. "In my office, having a quick checkup."

"Is he okay?"

"He seems to be. But he had a lot of faded bruising on his body when we found him."

Poor Tyler. "Was he beaten?"

"Yes. Probably by his father, the night before Ted reported the boy missing."

At that moment his office door opened and Dr. Marshall emerged with the young boy.

As soon as Tyler spotted Nessa, he broke out in a big smile.

"Nessa!"

He ran for her and she almost collapsed when she knelt to accept his embrace. As she hugged the little boy, she felt someone's hand at her back, steadying her. She glanced up and saw Dex watching her with a kind, slightly sad, expression.

Of course, it would have to be Dex.

"Oh, Tyler. I'm so happy to see you. Are you sure you're all right?" She pulled back from him, then gasped as she saw faded bruises on his face.

"Tyler's a healthy guy, thank goodness. I'll provide you with a written report later," the doctor informed Dexter. "And I'd like to see him in my office later in the week for a follow up examination."

Dex shook hands with the doctor. "Thank you for coming so quickly."

She gave him a curt nod. "No problem. But now I need to get to the clinic. One of my patients has gone into labor."

"That wouldn't be Rae Cordell?" Nessa was still crouched on the floor with Tyler. She didn't want to let the little boy go. The relief of finally being able to hold him was too sweet.

"Rae, it is," the doctor confirmed. "Wish me fortitude."

Nessa smiled, understanding exactly what she meant. Rae was a force to be reckoned with during the best of circumstances. Which childbirth probably wouldn't be.

"Come on, Tyler." Dex tried to extricate the child from Nessa's arms. "Let Nessa stand up, okay?"

"No." Tyler held on tighter, almost knocking her to the floor. Again, Dex was the one who gave her something to lean on. In this case, his legs.

"He's really attached to you," the lone female constable noted.

"He's one of my day care kids," Nessa explained. "A favorite, I have to admit. Come on, Tyler. Let's go sit on those chairs over there, okay?" She pointed to a corner, where a small seating area was set up around a coffeepot and a water cooler.

"I don't want you to go," the boy said, nestling his face into her shoulder.

"I'm not going anywhere, Tyler." Poor

baby. He had no one, now that his father had run off. No one.

"Come on, buddy. How about we go out for a hamburger?" Dex suggested. "Nessa will come, too, okay?"

Tyler looked at her to be sure. She nodded. "That's a great idea. I'm hungry, I didn't have any dinner. How about you, Tyler?"

"I'm hungry, too."

He let Dex lift him up onto his shoulders. Then Dex held out a hand to Nessa. She paused a moment, then placed her hand in his. He pulled, and when she was upright, held on a few extra seconds until she was steady.

"Need this?" The female constable handed her the walking stick, which had fallen to the floor when Tyler ambushed her.

"Thank you," Nessa said to both of them. She pulled back her hand from Dex. He was so kind to her. Even after she'd rejected him at the café. If only…

If only, what? She was healthy and could enter a relationship with him without any guilt? But if she hadn't become sick would she ever have found the strength to leave Gabe?

"Can I have a milk shake, too?" Tyler asked. "Please?"

Dex laughed. "You bet, Tyler. And fries, as well, if you want. Ready Nessa?"

"Sure." She led the way out of the bull pen, through the door that connected with the reception area. The police detachment was just across the road from Derby's Diner. She didn't want to go back there, not after the drama of the afternoon, but there weren't that many options for burgers and milk shakes on Summer Island.

Dex stepped ahead, opening the door for her, then asking for one of the booths in the corner. They ordered quickly and Tyler ate his food with obvious enjoyment.

Neither Nessa nor Dex made much of a dent in their own meals. Nessa sipped from her water glass, and watched Dex rub the stubble along his jawline. He looked so tired. At least now that Tyler had been found Dex would be able to get some rest and take time in the morning for a proper shave.

If circumstances had been different, she could be looking forward to a romantic dinner with him tomorrow night. Instead, she was afraid she'd just lost one of her best friends. Dex had barely looked at her this evening. He seemed to find the sight of her painful. Perhaps it was the walking cane.

When Tyler left the table to use the washroom, her gaze followed the little boy to the restroom door. "What's going to happen to him?" she asked quietly, keeping her eyes trained on the door.

Before Dex had a chance to reply, she already knew the answer.

"He'll go into foster care, won't he?"

"Probably."

Nessa wondered what that would be like. Would social services find a nice family for Tyler? However nice they might be, they would be strangers at first. And would the family live on the island, or would Tyler have to move to the mainland? Tyler had only ever lived one place in his life.

"I wish I could become a foster parent and offer him a home." She loved the children in her day care, but she craved more. A child of her very own.

"You could, you know," Dex said. "You'd have no trouble being accepted into the foster parent program."

"I wouldn't be so sure about that." She

grasped for her cane, then held it up for him to see. "What about this?"

"I don't get the problem."

"Dex, if I made a commitment to Tyler, I'd like it to be for the long term. But how can I promise to provide a home for him, when I can't be sure about my own health? For all I know, I'll be in a wheelchair next year."

Dex looked taken aback. "I've never heard you talk about your MS that way before. You've always been so optimistic.

"Like last year," he continued, "when you got the idea to start the day care. You were determined you weren't going to let MS stop you from making the most of your life."

"The day care's different. If I have to close shop one day, I'll be sad, but the children will be all right. Their parents will find alternative child care arrangements with little trouble. But I'm talking about becoming a parent here, Dex. Making a lifelong commitment. How can I do that, knowing I could let Tyler down?"

"A lifelong commitment," Dex muttered. "You mean like marriage?"

She rubbed her temples. "What does

marriage have to do with being Tyler's foster mom?"

Dex leaned over the table, his gaze direct and probing. "Is that why you turned me down this afternoon? I thought it had something to do with Gabe.... But it was the MS, wasn't it?"

"You deserve more than to be tied to a woman in a wheelchair."

"Oh, Nessa..."

Dex looked as if he would have said more, but just then Tyler returned from the washroom. The little boy yawned, obviously weary after his long day and his big meal.

Nessa held out her arms for a cuddle. Tyler came right to her. She held him tight and wondered how she'd ever let him go when the time came to place him with another family. "Can he stay with me tonight, Dex?"

"That's a good idea. I'll follow you in my car and help you get him settled."

"PUSH, RAE, PUSH!" Aidan was terrified. He had no idea what was going on and was merely parroting the instructions of the nurse and doctor.

"What do you think I'm doing, damn it? Knitting?"

Rae wouldn't take any guff, not even in the delivery room. He'd known she was a strong woman, but until tonight, he'd had no idea just how strong.

For some reason her labor had stalled shortly after they arrived at the clinic. She endured hours of what seemed to be endless contractions, all the while refusing any offer of pain relief.

Now, suddenly, the transition stage was over—whatever the hell transition was. He wished he'd been a little more prepared for this—because now it was time for the baby to come out.

Which meant pushing.

Whatever *that* was.

"Bear down, Rae," the nurse instructed. "Like going to the bathroom."

"This is so not like going to the bathroom," Rae shot back. Her hair was slick with sweat, her checks were apple-red. She gritted her teeth, grunted. Her cheeks grew even redder.

"I see the head!" Dr. Marshall sounded encouraged. "Give us a few more seconds…."

"I can't!" Rae let out her breath in a defeated whoosh.

"Oh, yes, you can," the nurse replied. "Take a moment to gather your strength. Come on, Dad," she urged him. "Cheer her on."

Desperate for something new to say, he went for the absurd. "Do it, Rae. Or I'll send you back to Pittsburgh."

She glared at him, then bore down again. Her face colored, her eyes strained.

"Come on, Rae. Come on! God, you're something else, woman. Do you know that?"

"We've got the top of the head," Dr. Marshall was cheering now, too. "Another push, Rae. Give us another one as strong as… Yes!"

Aidan had witnessed births on TV and in movies, but the reality was far more gory and gritty.

And miraculous.

A baby slid out into the doctor's waiting hands. A perfect, pink, beautiful baby.

"Was Annie right?" Rae collapsed back onto the delivery bed. She looked as if she'd just crossed a marathon line. Sweaty, exhausted…and also beautiful.

It took him a moment to find his voice. "Yes, Rae, Annie was right. You have a baby boy."

Aidan felt ecstatic just looking at him. *That's my boy. That's my son.*

And suddenly he realized how quiet the room had become. The nurse was cleaning the baby, weighing him, making notes on a chart by the baby's incubator. The doctor was palpating Rae's stomach gently, taking care of the afterbirth.

Both practitioners' expressions were solemn. No one said a word.

Then the nurse cocooned the baby in a blue blanket, so that only his little face was showing. She turned her back on him and Rae.

It was time, he realized bleakly.

They were going to take the baby away.

He remembered what Rae had said earlier. *I most definitely do not want to hold the baby.*

He looked down at her now and his heart, which had slowly begun to break, like ice cracking on a pond, spreading out from the point of impact in ever-widening circles, suffered another blow.

Her eyes were round with terror, her teeth were chattering, and he understood that her heart was breaking, too.

"Rae." He wanted to beg her not to do this. But for the first time he understood what this was costing her. If she thought she had to do this, then the least he could do was support her. He put his hand on her arm. "Don't watch. Close your eyes."

But she pushed him away. She pushed him away and sat upright on the bed, staring at the nurse who was holding their baby.

"Rae…" The doctor's voice was soothing. "Please lie down. I haven't finished—"

"Give me my baby."

"Rae?"

"Give me my baby. Now." The words came out deep and strong and full of authority. "Don't you dare take my baby away from me."

The nurse hesitated in the doorway. She was holding the baby in the crook of one arm. She glanced from Rae, to the doctor, then back to Rae. "You want to hold him, after all?"

"Hell, yes, I want to hold him." Rae held out her arms.

The nurse hesitated again, then brought the baby to the bed. Rae accepted the bundle greedily, bringing him close to her chest, clasping him to her heart.

"I'll never let you go," she whispered against the baby's head. "Never, never,

never." She closed her eyes and tears slid onto her cheeks. "I'll take parenting classes. I'll read every baby book I can get my hands on. I'll do my best, sweetheart. I promise, I'll do my best."

All the while she was making her vow to her son, she kept crying. And Aidan wished he had a video camera, because he didn't think he'd ever see anything this beautiful again in his entire lifetime.

And then she seemed to remember that he was still in the room. She opened her eyes and lifted her chin defiantly.

"You think I'm making a mistake?"

He pressed his finger against the baby's hand. His son's fingers splayed, then curved around his finger.

"No, Rae. This is no mistake. This is the best thing that ever happened to either of us."

CHAPTER TWENTY-ONE

NESSA THOUGHT DEX would leave once Tyler fell asleep, but he didn't. He prowled her living room, lifting objects such as her blown glass vase and peering under it, as if searching for clues.

He was stalling. Gathering his thoughts. Making her terribly nervous.

She settled on the sofa and flipped through the photographs she'd had developed today. Already she'd arranged the doubles into an album for Autumn so she would have a keepsake of their summer together. Maybe she should make another album for herself....

Suddenly Dex planted himself in the middle of the room, facing her. "Two weeks ago you didn't need a cane to walk."

She placed the pictures back inside the folder. "I know." She'd never expected her symptoms to worsen so dramatically, so quickly. "Next week I have an appointment in Seattle with my specialist. Maybe he can alter my meds...."

"I don't think you need more pills, Nessa. Two weeks ago is when Tyler went missing. You've been worried sick about him. Now that he's back, maybe you'll have a remission."

"It's possible. But not guaranteed."

"There are no guarantees about anything in life. But I don't see why we can't hope for the best. Even if you need a cane for the rest of your life, that doesn't mean you're headed for a wheelchair."

"That's true." MS was nothing if not unpredictable.

Dex sat down next to her and took her hands. "It's your life. I know that. But it just doesn't seem like you to live it assuming the worst-case scenario is going to occur."

His assessment stung. "That's not what I'm doing."

"Then why won't you apply to be Tyler's foster mom? If that's what you want."

"It *is* what I want."

"It would be the best thing for him, too.

Clearly, he's attached to you. That would make the transition easier."

"Yes."

Dex cleared his throat. "And if you had a husband, someone to be a father to Tyler, someone to take care of the house and mow the lawn, that sort of thing, it would be even better, don't you think?"

Nessa searched his eyes and saw sincerity. Kindness. He was such a good man, Dex Ulrich. But she couldn't let him do this. He didn't really understand what he might be sacrificing.

The idea of the three of them in the same house, a real family, was so beautiful she could cry. She'd never wanted more than that. A man who loved her. A child. A simple home near the sea.

But if she had two of the three, that would be enough.

"Dex, you would make a terrific father for Tyler. But you don't have to marry me to fulfill that role. You could take him to Boy Scouts, or play softball, or whatever it is that fathers and sons do together."

They could make it work, the three of them.

Dex could help Tyler so much, but he wouldn't need to give up his whole life to do it.

"Nessa you talk as if marrying you would be some big sacrifice on my part. That's crazy. Don't you know how much I love you? I've loved you for years."

"But I can't have children, Dex. Oh, it's possible, but pregnancy would be a strain on my body. One I'm not sure I'd want to risk. You'd never have your own daughter. Your own son."

"But I'd have you. I'd have Tyler. Maybe we'd apply for another foster child. Or adopt?"

Warmth flooded her, at the pictures his words created. She saw Dex in bed beside her every night. Saw him playing catch with Tyler. Maybe holding a baby? Wouldn't that be amazing…?

Then she imagined a completely different scenario. Herself in a wheelchair. Dex doing most of the work, running the household and raising Tyler. Then, a few years later she'd be in an institution and he'd feel obliged to visit her, adding yet another task to his already overloaded days….

"Oh, Dex. I'd like to believe in our future. But I'm so afraid that you'd end up sorry."

"Isn't that my choice to make?"

"But—"

"Nessa, there's only one thing you can say that would make me leave you."

She waited, afraid to hear what that one thing would be.

"Say you don't love me. Then I'll go."

She searched the depths of his eyes. "You know I can't say that."

"Then I'm here. And I'm not going anywhere."

RAE REMEMBERED Annie explaining that some women had trouble with breast-feeding, but she and her baby had no problem. Maybe Annie was right and she was a natural. Annie had been right about everything else, so why not?

She cuddled her son, stared dreamily down at his little face. His lips parted, releasing her nipple. He'd fallen asleep. She tucked her breast back inside the blue hospital gown and reclined against the pillows.

Aidan had rushed out to buy one of those disposable cameras from the gas station on the edge of town. It was the one store that was open past nine o'clock on the island.

He'd only been gone a couple of minutes, so she was surprised when someone tapped on her door.

"Who's there?" The nurse had just been in here. She'd said to call if Rae needed anything.

"How's the new mom?" Annie slipped into the room, her wrinkled face beaming.

"Annie." Thank God, Dex hadn't thrown her into jail. "Better late than never, I guess."

"Pshaw. I'm sure you didn't miss me."

"Of course, I missed you. But Aidan filled in not too badly for a man who doesn't have a clue about babies. You were right, by the way. We have a boy." She shifted the infant, so she could show off his sweet face.

"He's beautiful." Annie looked from the baby to Rae. "And you're going to make a terrific mother."

Rae felt herself flush. She hoped Annie was right about that. "Are you surprised I decided to keep him?"

Annie gave her an *are you kidding* look. Then she held out her arms. "Hand him over. I'm dying to cuddle a new baby."

Rae hadn't let go of him since the delivery. Well, once, for about five minutes, she'd let Aidan hold him. She definitely wasn't allowing the nurse anywhere near. She still harbored an irrational fear that they might force her to give him up.

She felt badly for the Thompsons. She had no illusions about the hurt that her decision would cause them. But the second her baby had been delivered, she'd known giving him up was utterly impossible.

The love had come in a tidal wave. And it had changed everything. Not only her decision, but her understanding of herself and the kind of person she'd been born to be.

"I suppose I can trust you." Gently she removed the baby and passed him over. Without him, she felt so cold. She shivered, then pulled up the blanket.

Annie cradled the baby to her sagging bosom. "Ah. This is just what I needed."

One day ago, Rae wouldn't have understood. Now she knew exactly how the former midwife felt. "But why are you here? Dex was so angry, I was sure you'd be spending the night in his interrogation room."

"That's been taken care of."

"Oh?"

Annie let out a long sigh. "Here's the

official story. I'm an old, confused woman who doesn't read the newspapers. I didn't realize everyone on the island was searching for the little boy. As soon as I found out, I contacted the authorities and let them know Tyler was fine."

Rae laughed. Annie was clearly insulted by the slur on her mental acuity, but presumably she'd rather be humiliated than in jail facing kidnapping charges.

"But what about the letter you sent to Ted Jenkins?"

"Letter?" Annie's eyebrows arched in puzzlement. "What letter?"

So Dex Ulrich had destroyed it. He was a good man, Rae decided.

The door to her room opened again, and Aidan came rushing inside. "I've got a camera!"

He stopped short at the sight of Annie. "You're not in jail?"

With another sigh, Annie handed the baby back to Rae. "It's a long story. Rae will tell you all about it. But first give me that camera and go sit by Rae. We'd better start taking pictures before this kid learns to walk. And by the way—I'm going to want a copy."

ANNIE TOOK SEVERAL SHOTS of the three of them before handing the camera back to Aidan. "Okay, I have to go home. I haven't had Jennifer's lecture yet, and I suppose my brother will have to get in a few words, too."

Rae hoped Annie's family wouldn't be too hard on her. Annie had taken a big risk for Tyler's sake. Would anyone else have dared to do what she had done?

Annie left and somehow the room became smaller. Aidan was still sitting next to Rae on the bed. Without saying a word, he slipped off his shoes and put up his feet. He lifted his arm, creating a space for her and she leaned into it. She could feel his warmth, as well as the baby's. They were all touching now. Aidan had his hand resting on the baby's back, and the baby was cuddled up to her breast.

How cozy it was. Like a nest.

Suddenly, Rae realized she was tired. She let her head relax against Aidan's shoulder. Closed her eyes.

Now she became aware of sounds. Mostly breathing. Was it her, Aidan, the baby, or all three of them? She knew the baby was breathing. She could actually feel his lungs empty and fill in a reassuringly steady rhythm.

Her baby was fine. He was here. Safe.
She fell asleep.

RAE OPENED HER EYES and instantly thought about her baby. "Where is he?" She bolted upright in the bed, patting the covers. How could she have dropped him?

"He's fine, Rae. Relax."

Aidan was reclined in a chair next to her bed. He had the baby in his arms. He'd draped a blanket over his chest and the baby's cheek rested against it.

Rae's adrenaline stopped surging. "He's breathing?"

"Constantly. It's, like, never-ending."

She wouldn't smile. You didn't joke about things like this. "Is he hungry? What time is it? How often am I supposed to feed him?"

God, she didn't know *anything*. She had to get online and order every parenting book Amazon had in stock.

"I'm guessing he'll let us know when he wants to eat," Aidan said.

How could he sound so calm?

"Well, we ought to be doing *something*."

"I changed his diaper a while ago. Really,

I think all we need to do right now is enjoy him. Would you like to hold him?"

Enjoy him. That was good advice. Maybe it was the best advice of all. She held out her arms, marveling at how right he felt in her arms.

Had she ever felt right in her mother's arms? Had her mother ever enjoyed having a baby, a daughter?

Rae didn't think so.

That was one mistake she wouldn't make. She was going to treasure every day of this child's life. There would be other mistakes to watch out for, though. Later, when she was home, she would make a list of all the things she would never do.

Like call him a mistake. Or blame him for her unhappiness. Or rue the day that he'd been born.

Or curse his father...

She glanced over at Aidan. He was watching her—watching them both—with the dopiest smile on his face. She pressed her own lips together, afraid she would end up with the exact same expression.

"This has been quite an evening," Aidan said.

"It's quarter to midnight. In fifteen minutes, our boy will be officially one day old."

Our boy. Rae swallowed. "He's really perfect, isn't he?"

"Just like his mother," Aidan agreed.

"Perfect is something I'll never be." Her mother had made her feel worthless growing up, but Rae knew her good points. She was smart, a savvy businessperson, an honest person in general.

But she was aware of her flaws, as well. Too outspoken at times. Okay, a lot of the time. There were probably other flaws, but she was too tired to think of them right now.

She kissed the top of her baby's head, then blinked as the camera flashed bright.

"That'll be a great picture," Aidan said.

She was glad he'd taken it. Would there be other pictures of her with her son? On his first birthday, his first day of school, his graduation?

If so, who would take them?

She looked at Aidan again, realizing there was so much they needed to talk about. "Keeping the baby wasn't my plan. It'll change everything."

Aidan nodded, and Rae wondered what he was thinking. Would he want to be part of the baby's life? That meant they'd need to live in the same city. She should tell him he didn't need to transfer to Pittsburgh. She opened her mouth, but before she could get out the words, Aidan was already talking.

"We'll have to get married."

"What?" Hadn't they covered this route already? "That isn't a good idea. A baby isn't a strong enough foundation for a marriage."

Aidan moved closer. Took her hand. "He wouldn't be. Rae, do you know what you need? I think I do."

She waited to hear.

"Someone who loves you and wants you. Not because you're the mother of their baby, not because you're a kick-ass negotiator, but because you're you. For no other reason than because of you."

She held her breath, mesmerized by his words because they were so true. She wanted the impossible, what she'd never had. Someone who loved her, Rae Cordell, with no strings attached.

"And you know what, Rae? You've got that. Because that's how I feel about you. Love will be our foundation, Rae. And Layton—"

She blinked. "Layton?"

He put a hand on their baby's head. "That's my mother's maiden name. Our son—Layton—he's our very wonderful signing bonus."

It was a lot to take in. A lot to process. She gazed into Aidan's eyes, looking for the smallest hint that he didn't mean every word he'd just said.

She could see only sincerity.

"I've loved you since that night in Philadelphia," she told him, laying her heart bare for the first time in her life. "Let's name him Layton Cordell Wythe."

"Agreed."

Aidan leaned forward to kiss her on the lips. She caught his hand and held it tight. Never in her life had she sealed a sweeter deal.

* * * * *

*Return to Summer Island one more time
in October 2006 to read
Jennifer March's story,
SECRETS BETWEEN THEM (SR #1375)!*

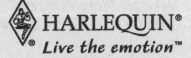

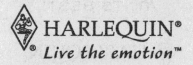

HARLEQUIN®
INTRIGUE®

WE'LL LEAVE YOU BREATHLESS!

If you've been looking for thrilling tales of
contemporary passion and sensuous love stories
with taut, edge-of-the-seat suspense—then
you'll love Harlequin Intrigue!

Every month, you'll meet six new heroes
who are guaranteed to make your spine tingle
and your pulse pound. With them you'll enter
into the exciting world of Harlequin Intrigue—
where your life is on the line
and so is your heart!

THAT'S INTRIGUE—
ROMANTIC SUSPENSE
AT ITS BEST!

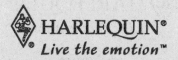

HARLEQUIN®
Live the emotion™

HARLEQUIN®
Presents

The world's bestselling romance series...
The series that brings you your favorite authors,
month after month:

Helen Bianchin...Emma Darcy
Lynne Graham...Penny Jordan
Miranda Lee...Sandra Marton
Anne Mather...Carole Mortimer
Susan Napier...Michelle Reid

and many more uniquely talented authors!

Wealthy, powerful, gorgeous men...
Women who have feelings just like your own...
The stories you love, set in exotic, glamorous locations...

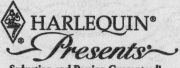

HARLEQUIN®
Presents

Seduction and Passion Guaranteed!

Harlequin Historicals®
Historical Romantic Adventure!

*From rugged lawmen and
valiant knights to defiant heiresses
and spirited frontierswomen,
Harlequin Historicals will
capture your imagination with
their dramatic scope, passion
and adventure.*

*Harlequin Historicals . . .
they're too good to miss!*